CUTTING EDGE

The Edge - Prequel

CD REISS

Cutting Edge

A prequel to the Edge Series

A world of thanks to my fellow authors, Rebecca Yarros and Sarah Fergusen, whose lives have been shaped by love for men and women in military service. Their patience in explaining military culture resulted in as much accuracy as you see here. The mistakes are probably plenty and all mine.

This book is dedicated to the men and women of the US military.

I wish I'd known more about what you do, not so writing this book would be easier, but because it's my duty.

Part One

Chapter One

NOVEMBER, 2004
THE AIR OVER FALLUJAH, IRAQ
18 HOURS TO OPERATION PHANTOM FURY

NOT JUMPING.

I chanted two words to myself over and over.

Not jumping.

The Phrog's dual rotors buzzed like a swarm of bees. My knuckles were striated in white and pink, and my palm already ached in the center. I kept my eyes on my boots and focused on the pain, feeling it in three dimensions as the shooting ache ran from my right wrist to my shoulder. That helped. Focusing on pain always did.

"How you doing, Major?"

3

I barely heard Ronin over the angry swarm and the shouts of the paratroopers, but I couldn't ignore him. That was as good as an admission of the terror I felt. He'd use my fear as a weapon for good-natured but annoying mockery. Any woman with thirteen years in the military could take a ribbing, but none of us had to like it.

He was on the other side of the cargo bay, right next to the rear dock. I looked at him and released my hand long enough to give him a thumbs-up, but I couldn't do that without seeing the open bay door the paratroopers were jumping from.

My stomach twisted when I saw the rectangle of clear blue desert sky and watched the marine sergeant smack a soldier on the helmet before she jumped and disappeared.

Ronin laughed. He was a loaner from Intelligence, temporarily attached to my unit in the First Medical Brigade. He was an ass, a friend, and an occasional bunk buddy since we'd met in basic training.

"One day you're gonna have to jump," he shouted.

I kept my hand up long enough to give him the finger, then I clutched the edge of my seat again.

"Cork it!" Lieutenant Jackson shouted to him, her eyes intent under her thick, black glasses. Jenn was a nurse practitioner and my best friend in the unit.

Ronin smiled at her. She had a silver bar to his butterbar. He couldn't do shit.

The sergeant smacked himself on the helmet and jumped out.

Next stop: Combat Support Hospital—Balad Base.

The door was closed, and the helicopter whipped around, pressing my back against the fuselage.

WE ARRIVED AT THE CSH, combat support hospital, in the brightest part of the day. Sweat had a way of burning right off you between noon and two in July in Iraq, and what didn't burn off, the wind took away. But in November, the dusty landscape of the airbase sat in contrast to the temperate air. I was on my third deployment, and I'd seen every season in the Middle East. Fall was my favorite.

"They have eighteen surgeons." Our CO, Colonel Brogue, briefed us in the truck to base. "Six are US Army. Two are Aussie. Ten are Air Force."

We were a team of sixteen medical officers: Two general surgeons. Two doctors. Eleven nurses. And me, a psychiatrist. Brogue had gone ahead of us and come back. He'd been a medic in Bosnia and Kosovo and now ran our medical unit. We'd all been reassigned to Balad ahead of a push into Fallujah —because nothing creates an unmanageable number of casualties like a push into battle.

"Do they have their own psych team?" I asked.

"Not at present." Brogue was in his sixties with tight, white hair and a chest built like a cinderblock wall. Old school. He thought real men didn't need mental health specialists but could probably have used one himself. "It's all you, and we're headed into a major offensive. We need you focused on keeping the surgeons sharp."

Not healthy. Sharp. Welcome to the army in wartime.

"Yes, sir," I said.

I saw Ronin in my peripheral vision, nodding. I wondered what he was doing here, but he'd never say until he had to.

We blew by corrugated metal trailers used for housing and more permanent plywood structures that had been there when the base was run by the Iraqi Air Force.

As everyone got off the truck, I said to Brogue privately, "I'd like to meet the surgeons first. I'd like to have an idea of how they handle stress before the choppers start landing. Can we set up intakes?"

"Army guys, sure. Air Force has to go through their command."

"Got it."

I got out of the back of the truck. We were in front of a tin hangar with tents being erected on each side. The gravity of the situation became clear with the sight of those tented areas. The hospital wasn't big enough for what was coming.

The sky was crystalline blue, heavy and thick, the only pure thing in a messy world. It connected all of us equally under its sapphire bowl.

Its presence disconcerted me, and yet there was hope under it.

HE WAS the last of the six army surgeons. Captain Caden St. John. Accepted a commission after finishing Officer Candidate School in November 2001. Desperate for general surgeons, the army had signed him to a three-year commission and a four-year service obligation. Field training at Walter Reed. He'd just started his second sixteen-month deployment. I was surprised he'd lasted this long. He was still a civilian as far as I was concerned.

"Jenn." I caught Lt. Jackson as she set up triage in one of the tents.

"Yeah," she grunted, moving the monitor on a crash cart.

I helped her move the cart. "I'm looking for Dr. St. John?"

"The hot one?"

"By 'hot' you mean...?"

"On fire. He just got out of the OR."

Strange. Casualties hadn't come in yet. I knotted my brow and headed for the changing room.

Metal sinks. Empty linen hampers. One man in scrubs stood with his back to me, peeling off bloody gloves.

"Dr. St. John?"

"Yeah?" He slipped off his cap, revealing a full head of dark hair.

"I'm Dr. Frazier from psych."

He pulled off his scrubs and his undershirt in one movement, and I had to bite back a gasp. I'd seen some pretty ripped soldiers, but he'd caught me by surprise. His waistband hung on his hips below two divots in his lower back. Surgeons didn't look like that.

"Psychiatrists don't fucking knock?"

"Surgeons don't close the fucking door?"

He turned at the waist—just enough to take stock of me. His jaw was sketched with a light beard, his lips were a full, dusty pink, his eyebrows arched, and his eyes... his fucking eyes were the color of the bowl that connected all of us.

Were my nipples hard?

Maybe. He didn't linger on them though. He took inventory slowly and deliberately, giving equal weight to my feet, my legs, my torso, before landing on my face.

"You wanted something?" he asked, turning around again and undoing the tie at his waistband.

"There's an offensive coming," I said.

"No shit." He dropped his pants.

His ass was too perfect for human eyes. I looked away.

"I need to do a benchmark intake on your mental state. It's going to get hairy around here real soon."

Smiling, he turned around, giving me the full sight of an

enormous cock. He balled his scrubs and tossed them in a hamper beside me. I kept my focus off his dick and on his eyes, but they were doorways to the sky and I was afraid of heights.

"I'll be fine," he said, picking up his camo shirt by the neck. The name tape said JOHN without the ST., and his rank was on his collar.

"Captain," I replied, "I'll see you at my desk in one hour, ready to answer questions."

He smiled like a fucking civilian. His dimples went black with his beard, and his eyes sparkled as if the sky could rain without clouds. "Of course."

I put my right toe behind my left heel, spun, and about-faced before he could see his effect on my body.

WITH A FOOTBALL TUCKED under his arm, Ronin ran like an All-American. I waited until he spiked it in the end zone before I stopped him.

"How are the intakes?" he asked.

"Almost done. Now it's just hurry up and wait." I scraped my foot on the sand. It sparkled.

"Broken glass?" he asked.

"Mortar fire melts sand into glass." I pointed toward the border of the base. "They shoot them over the wire."

He tossed the ball to his teammates. "Fun times."

"No joke." I nodded, and he took two steps back toward the game.

"Wanna hang out before the shit hits the fan?" he asked.

We both knew what he meant by "hang out," and I couldn't. No reason not to really, except... I couldn't. Not with the sky watching.

"I have nursing and support staff to interview," I said. "Maybe next war."

MY DESK WAS two sawhorses with a slab of plywood laid across. I had a small, barely private office separated from triage by white canvas walls.

Ronin didn't have a desk. He stood at mine and handed me a metal box. "You should hang on to this."

"What is it?" I opened the box to find vials of clear liquid.

"Synthetic amphetamine."

"We have plenty of the generic." I went over the contraindications. To be used after rest, no food required, eight-hour spread.

Ronin shrugged. "Works faster and stays effective longer. One shot holds twenty-four hours."

I folded up the sheet and stuck it back in the box. "What are you doing here anyway?"

"I can neither confirm nor deny I'm even in Fallujah."

"I won't tell then."

He smiled and left to do whatever it was he did.

Fifty-nine minutes after I left post-op, Caden poked his head around the canvas flap of my office. He was fully covered in camo, thank God, and he'd shaved.

"Major," he said with a smirk, as if he found my title arousing.

"Greyson's fine." I indicated the chair in front of my makeshift desk.

He sat in it, slipping off his cap, which told me volumes. A gentleman by training. Strict, traditional upbringing. His behavior in the post-op room had been deliberate and against character.

"Thank you for the show in post-op," I said.

"It's a changing room. You can't be shocked I was changing."

"It takes more than a penis to shock me." *Even a magnificent one.*

"A quality I admire."

The parentheses around his smile were no less effective without the beard.

"The schedule says you were doing a hernia operation."

"Real quick. I just needed two surgical nurses and a gasser."

"And the patient?"

"He's fine."

"You couldn't put it off for a few days?"

"Why?"

Why? meant *why not?* Like asking a four-year-old why he'd had the extra lollipop. Why not watch an extra hour of TV? Why postpone joy?

Mental note: *He loves it. Expect him to engage in risk-taking behavior and attempt to function even if performance is suffering. Expect him to push his limits in the OR.*

"In an emergency," I said, taking out the five-page mental evaluation questionnaire, "we may have to administer psychotropic medications before we can evaluate their safety for you. So, we do this assessment before we need to."

I pushed the questionnaire toward him. He put his elbows on my desk and flipped through it.

"About the changing room," I said.

"You see something you like?" He snapped up a pen and ticked boxes.

"Why did you feel the need to express your dominance over a woman you didn't even know?"

Head still facing the page, he looked me with only his eyes. "I was getting changed."

"Denial is a river in Egypt, Captain."

He went back to the questions, reading and answering quickly. "Caden's fine." He showed me the page. "What exactly do you mean here?" He tapped the pen on a question. "Forty-seven. Part B. Does jerking off count?"

Why was my neck going prickly? I talked about deviant sex acts with attractive patients all the time. Many transferred sexual feelings onto me, and I was trained to deal with it. This guy had disarmed me completely.

"Sexual activity is with a partner. Masturbation is covered in question forty-nine."

"Ah." He put the paper down and, on question 47b, ticked the box for "infrequently."

One. He hadn't fucked the entire camp, male and/or female.

Two. He'd made sure I saw which box he ticked.

I watched him move over the last page, his answers marked with Xs that went from corner to corner without overshooting the boundaries. His hand was wide across the knuckles with long fingers and had a way of moving that was like a lucid, articulate speech pattern. Every stroke counted.

What would those hands feel like on my body?

Cool air came into contact with the sweat breaking out on my neck. I pretended to reread medication labeling while he finished, but I kept his hand in view over the edge of the page.

He put down the pen and pushed the papers toward me.

CD REISS

"Thank you, Caden."

"My pleasure."

I stood, then he stood. "I'll let you know if I have any follow-up questions."

He transferred his cap from his right to his left and held out his right hand. "Nice to meet you."

That hand bridged more than a gap in rank. That. Beautiful. Hand.

I took it, and we shook.

He turned to leave but stopped at the flap just as I was sitting. "So you know, in the changing room? My ass was because I was annoyed that you came in. I showed you the rest because I want to fuck you."

My pussy clenched as if he'd kissed it. "That is highly inappropriate."

"I know." He put on his cap and left.

NO DISCIPLINARY ACTIONS. No insubordination. No complaints at all.

Caden St. John had a year and a quarter left on his obligation. He didn't owe the army time for his education. If he left at the end of his four years, he wouldn't get a pension, but from his

14

sweet reek of privilege, I got the feeling he wasn't worried about that.

I'd been active duty for almost thirteen years. The obligation I'd accrued for my medical training would be paid in two years. He'd be long gone by then. Not that it mattered.

Not that it mattered at all.

Seven and half months between the end of his obligations and mine.

Why would I even do that math?

From my trailer, I heard the transports rumbling. Boots stomped on the pavement. Rifles click-clacked, and men yelled orders.

They were heading out.

There was nothing I could do now. I'd prepared as much as I could. I tried to rest, lying on my back with my hands folded across my chest. In the space between sleep and wakefulness, when the dark part of my heart opened like a simply written birthday card, I wished I could go with them.

Chapter Two

DAY ONE

04:06:00

Meal scheduling was suspended. The chow hall had laid out some basics to keep everyone going. The usual laughter and conversation at the long tables had also been put on hold apparently. Anyone staying still long enough to eat was working or filling out requisition forms. I was sitting with the brass, huddled at a round table by the soda machine.

The tension of anticipation was butter-thick.

"One good thing about an offensive," Colonel Brogue said, fisting a hot burrito, then chomping off the end like a jerky stick. "Enemy doesn't have the time or people to hit us. This base normally gets a mortar a week. Now it's crickets."

"Any idea how long it could go? I calculated shifts for the medical staff, but it breaks down after forty-eight hours," I said.

"Gonna need more than that." He balled up the burrito wrapper and got rid of it with a cocksure toss that landed right in the pail. He must have been a complete stud when he first got his commission.

"I can extend it. Rotate in more rest. Four days sound right?"

We walked out of chow hall and into the buzzing night.

"These people are fighting for their lives. Our guys are fighting for fuck-all for anyone can figure out."

I'd heard this in my sessions. Wounded soldiers wondered what they'd given their bodies for. They were snide or angry, but few broke down. Your mental state was the measure of your worth as a soldier. Anger was acceptable. Weakness was not. They were a hard lot to heal.

The colonel stopped between the motor pool and the hospital. Interior lights enveloped a swarm of activity, bleeding together in the open space between.

"You're from California, right, Major Frazier?" he asked.

"My father was in the 101st Airborne, so we moved a lot. He and mom retired to San Diego."

"Yeah, well, I don't know what's on your minds out there. But if someone air-dropped onto Main Street and said they were running shit, I'm sure you wouldn't take too kindly. You'd fight to the death."

"It's like you know me."

He wagged his finger at me. "I know a soldier when I see one."

"Thank you, sir."

"So, when you make your rotations, keep that in mind."

"I will. Thank you."

DAY ONE
08:23:00

THE SURGICAL ROTATIONS were set at six days. Without a full day's rest, they'd start breaking down at four days, and the mistakes would start. After that, we'd need more doctors and nurses. We had enough PAs for an extra twelve hours. It wouldn't be enough, because if tanks full of foreign soldiers rolled down Main Street, I'd fight to the death.

There was a shout outside as a truck pulled up.

I went out through the hospital. Boxes were being unloaded, and I was nearly knocked over by a grunt carrying a crate of meds.

"Sorry," he shouted over his shoulder.

"No pro—"

A weight hit my chest, pushing me back. I spun back to front and center.

It was still night, but the bright light of day shone in Caden's eyes. He pushed the crate against me. "Take it."

I held my arms out under the crate and accidentally touched his hands. He slid them out from under, giving me the full weight.

"Give it to Yvonne," he said. "She knows where it goes."

Without another word, he went back to the truck, scrubs skimming his body until he was naked in my mind.

"Let's go!" a sergeant shouted to someone I couldn't see. It didn't matter. Time to get moving.

I found Yvonne and gave her the crate, then I went for another, taking whatever was handed to me.

Twice more, the hauling pattern brought us together. Twice more, our hands brushed together under the box. After the second time, I returned to the loading dock to find the truck pulling away. Caden watched it go with his bare arms crossed in the cold air. On most men, that body language was closed. On him, the ropes of his forearms were nothing if not inviting.

"Did they bring additional staff?" I asked.

"Nope. They took two surgical nurses though."

"What? Who?"

"Barn Door and Guitterez." Totally normal to pepper nicknames with real names. "They have field experience."

"Shit."

He raised an eyebrow at me, tilting his body in my direction.

I stepped back toward my office. "I have to watch the nurses too."

"That's about to be the least of our problems. Rumor has it, at least."

"It'll be fine."

"Sure." Before I could get back to the tent, he called for me. "Major."

I turned on the ball of my foot. He was the only still point in the floodlight. "Yeah?"

"I was being a dick. No excuses."

"It's all right."

"Under different circumstances though..." He didn't finish.

"If wishes were horses, Captain."

"The streets would be full of horseshit."

I laughed. He was pulled back into the hospital with a wave. I went to redo my rotation forecasting, imagining meeting him in a different situation, a different time, a different place.

DAY ONE

09:12:00

WHEN THE CHOPPERS ARRIVED, there was a palpable

sense of relief among the staff. They had jobs and could finally do them. I didn't have much for the first few hours. I fetched and ran. Filled in forms. Administered first aid when needed. Assisted as much as I could. I was an MD, but the best use of my skills was to let people who knew what they were doing get the job done.

That was the report I wrote in my head.

The reality of triage was more complex.

"Major Frazier!" Corporal LeShawn called. He was kneeling by a screaming man bathed in black soot and blood, holding a red-soaked gauze over the soldier's hip.

I ran over because I was needed, but my chest hitched, and I had to hold back a cry of despair over his pain. It wasn't the first time that day I'd had to enforce professional detachment—or the last. I navigated rows of bloody stretchers, narrowly missed a nurse heading in the opposite direction, and kneeled across from the corporal, trying to breathe around the stench of intestinal matter.

"Pressure," he said calmly.

Surprised I could hear him through the screams, I replaced his hands on the bloody gauze while he put together a morphine drip. The wounded soldier was down to weeping.

"You're doing great," I said, checking his blood-soaked name tape. "Hardy. You're doing great. Breathe."

"They came out of nowhere. I didn't see them."

"You did your best."

"They were everywhere." He was hyperventilating from the memory.

"Okay, breathe." His hand grabbed for mine, and I took it. "You're here now. LeShawn's getting you something for the pain."

The drip was going.

"My wife." An injured man will often forget the strength he has in the limbs that still work, and Hardy had forgotten his hands could probably break mine. "We run marathons. If I can't run… will I be able to run?"

I didn't know if he had anything worse than a paper cut or if he was too wounded to walk again.

Outside, the slapping sound of choppers. More coming.

"I'm not that kind of doctor."

"Doctor Frazier!" a voice called from behind me.

"Don't go!" Private Hardy grabbed me with his other hand, clutching my forearm.

"Major! We need you!"

I pulled away, the blood acting as a lubricant between our hands.

"I'll come see you in recovery," I said, trying to get his fist off my forearm.

"Don't go. Please."

I didn't want to go. I wanted to crouch by him for as long as he needed me, but hands appeared, pulling him off me, and before I could think about Private Hardy, I was holding a stitch tray, and before I could check on whether he'd made it to the OR, I was cutting away a bloody pant leg, and before I could think about eating or going to the latrine to relieve the painful pressure on my bladder, I was holding another man's hand as a brain injury metastasized into death.

DAY ONE
14:39:00

ENFORCING rest and nutrition was hard, especially with the surgeons. One in particular.

"I'm not changing out, eating a bag of chips, and scrubbing back in." Caden plucked a bit of shrapnel out of a pink gut and dropped it in a plastic tray. A nurse held up the X-ray against the light. He peered at it. "Let's get the one in the ilium."

The nurse repeated the order, and hands moved over the table.

"All you have to do is stand still for a second," I said. I'd scrubbed in to work with him and Dr. Indira, the other surgeon. She was generally easier to talk to.

"Really?" He squinted around the body, looking for a piece of something that shouldn't have been there.

"Really."

"Give me a little room here," he said to the nurse. "I think I got it."

"You're not afraid of a shot, are you?"

He glanced up from the wounded soldier, just a set of blue eyes over the gray rectangle of his surgical mask. "Where?"

"Intramuscular."

His eyebrows, which seemed darker and more curved without the distraction of his mouth, went up a fraction of an inch. "Go for it."

I got behind him and put my tray on a stand.

"Take your time," he said. "Can you clean that up for me?" he said in a completely different tone.

"I have six other surgeons with depleted blood sugar," I said, pulling his pants away from the smallest patch of skin possible. "I don't need to waste time on your ass."

I wished I could because as I estimated the midpoint between his side and the crack of his ass, quickly feeling for the curve of his bone, I decided it was the only worthy ass I'd ever touched. After swiping an alcohol wipe over the site, I stretched the skin and gave him his shot.

"All done." I covered him.

"What did you give me?"

"Glucose and B vitamins."

"Boring." Another piece of shrapnel clicked in the tray.

"We're saving the good stuff."

"I'll be here."

DAY TWO
23:02:00

NONE of the surgeons had rested. Half the triage group had taken a catnap. The nurses, who as a profession understood they were the lynchpin of the team, were keeping to their rest schedule when possible.

"We haven't had a chopper in three hours," Colonel Brogue said over hot coffee and rolls that had come sealed in noisy plastic. "If we hold, everyone can get a little shuteye before the next round."

"They're going to start breaking down in twelve hours." Looking over the hunched, tired figures haunting the chow hall, I figured I was being generous.

"What about you?"

"I got an hour this afternoon. I have four men in recovery I'm keeping an eye on."

I couldn't say more without betraying a confidence. They were suicidal, depressed, suffering from acute emotional exhaustion, and pretending they were fine. Hardy, the marathoner, was on his second deployment. Another was an Iraqi translator who only wanted to be comforted in Arabic, a language I spoke well enough to make me feel a responsibility toward him.

I spent more time with the lightest wounds. The men who could be sent back into combat were the ones I could do the most good for. I could recommend they be sent home. The others would be sent back to the States whether they had PTSD or not.

"They're soldiers," Brogue said. "This is their job. You can take care of them later. Keep the doctors awake. This ain't over." He shook his head pensively and said half to himself, "I wish I could get back out there."

DAY THREE
13:43:00

CADEN ST. JOHN WAS A MACHINE. The morning of the second day, we'd moved from vitamins and glucose to a cocktail of shots that included caffeine and an over-the-counter stimulant. He didn't stop. His joints were swollen. He denied any pain in his shoulders. He was lying.

They kept coming and coming.

As long as he wasn't shaking or losing motor skills, he was to stay in the OR.

And they kept coming. By truck and chopper, with flesh wounds and worse, they came. The smell of blood was now so hooked in my nostrils I didn't even notice it. The cloy of alcohol smelled clean instead of sharp, and when I went outside, the cold air seemed so hollow it jabbed my sinuses.

I took naps when I could. By the third day, they were little more than a necessary inconvenience, and their ability to refresh me diminished with each passing rotation.

And still, Caden worked as if he was in secret competition with the other surgeons. They rested when they could. He changed out when he had to use the latrine and scrubbed right back in.

I shot him up every eight hours with vitamins and stimulants, and on day three, I went to the next level.

"Amphetamine?" he asked as he turned on the faucet to scrub in.

I held up the syringe in my latex-coated hand. "It's that or go to bed."

He looked me up and down with red-rimmed eyes. "Since both involve you taking my pants down, I'll pick... eenie, meenie, miney..."

"The speed," I said, getting behind him. "You'll take the speed or a nap with your pants on."

"Crank it up."

We were alone. Not that it mattered for him. It mattered for me. I didn't want to enjoy touching his bottom, but if I did and it showed, I didn't want anyone to see.

After exposing a patch of skin, I ripped open an alcohol wipe. "What's driving you?"

"The guys on the table."

"Don't lie to me." I jabbed him with the needle.

"Wow, tired, Doctor? You're a little punchy."

I wiped blood off. "I've spent two days looking at your ass. I think I deserve an honest answer. You jumped into the military after 9/11. Okay, fine. You're not the first. But you've got more defense mechanisms than the Pentagon, and you do this job like you're digging out of a hole someone's shoveling dirt into."

When he looked over his shoulder, I realized I was still wiping his bottom with the swab. I cleared my throat and pulled up his pants.

He turned with his hands pointed up at the elbows. "Gown."

I got a gown off the shelf and ripped open the package, careful not to touch the outside of the sterile garment.

"You're not winning," I said, holding up the sterile garment. "No one wins this."

He slid his hands through the armholes, and I draped it over his shoulders. When my arms met behind his neck, I identified his scent. Fresh coffee grounds and the cut grass of a suburban Saturday morning.

"My parents were in the North Tower," he said softly, as if his words needed to be padded with seduction. "Hundred and first floor. They fell for about ten seconds, reaching a velocity of almost one hundred thirteen miles per hour. Fully conscious the whole way down. And when they hit, the force transferred all the energy they'd accumulated over those ten seconds outward. They never identified which grease spots were theirs. But they did find one of my mother's shoes."

I opened my mouth to give condolences, but his lips stopped me. He didn't kiss me but put them against mine, transferring his words into my throat.

"My father wasn't a good person." I felt the scrape of his chapped lower lip as it moved. "He was a sadistic monster, and none of these kids are going to die for his sake."

"And your mother?"

We kept our eyes open as he brushed his lips against mine, running their circumference, and with every turn, my body hungered for more. A true kiss. The taste of his tongue. The flutter of his eyelids when they closed. A murmur of desire in his throat.

But he didn't offer that, nor did he attribute any of his motivations to his mother.

"Close it please," he whispered.

My face went hot with shame. I shut my mouth and tied the loops at the back of his neck. He turned, hands still above his waist, so I could close him up in the back. My heart was still pounding, and the space between my legs had gone swollen and heavy.

"You owe me a story," he said.

"Once upon a time, there was a handsome prince. He wanted to woo the fair lady, but he was a jerk, and she had no time for it. So, he moved on to someone else. The end." I patted him, done with the last tie.

He turned. "Your story."

"That is my story."

"It's not finished." He pulled on a glove as a new shift burst in to scrub.

The room exploded into activity, but he and I were in our own little world.

"How do you know?" I got a mask ready for him.

"It ended with what he did, not what she did." As he snapped on the second glove, the *pah-pah* of chopper blades rose in the distance. "No pressure." He bowed his head. I looped the mask around his neck, and he stood straight. "None of us know how our story ends. Shit, we don't even know how this mess all ends...or when."

"You always get philosophical when you're tired?"

"I like you. I'm tired enough to say that and mean it. And I want to know your story."

"That's the amphetamine talking." I put the mask over his face.

"If you say so." He backed away, hands still up.

I called out before he went through the doors to the OR. "Maybe I'll tell it to you if you're good."

Under his mask, he smiled.

Chapter Three

DAY FOUR
16:23:00

I spoke to every soldier in recovery. Most of them told their stories with a healthy serving of bravado and swagger. I listened for hours on end, doling out sleeping pills, anti-depressants, and when allowed, comfort. I heard a hundred war stories told like the final minutes of a football game that was won or lost. But sadness was not allowed. Weakness was a disease. More than half wanted to go back to the front to join or avenge their buddies.

My father had been nineteen in 1968. He was a retired staff sergeant who never mentioned Vietnam. Not when my brother signed up, nor when I did. He only talked about the years he spent training soldiers Stateside, as if we didn't know why we had to knock before we entered a room he was in or why he woke up shouting, "They're all dying!" in the middle of the night.

And still, we joined because it was what our family did.

I'd never seen a battle, nor had I seen the back end of it until Balad. Casualties kept coming. I got a few hours' sleep when I could, but they kept coming, and they needed me as much as they needed the surgeons. One screaming soldier was rolled under them as a stitched-up one was rolled away. Surgeons grabbed an hour of sleep until the next chopper. But not Caden. He was shredding his brain, and I was helpless to do anything for him except fill him full of vitamins and speed.

"He stopped joking around three hours ago." I peered through the window in the OR door. "Hasn't spoken except to ask for instruments."

"You're obsessed," Ronin said from next to me.

Understatement of the year.

"What he's doing... it's not even heroic at this point. It's suicide. So, yes. I'm obsessed with stopping it."

"He has a commanding officer."

"Who wants results."

"They can get MPs in here to haul him away."

I shook my head, watching Caden sew up an internal organ cut open by bullets. No one was hauling him away. They'd work him until he was dead.

"We should break into the stuff I brought from the Pentagon. It's labeled for performance under exhaustion."

"It's also labeled to be taken after resting."

"Maybe that'll get him to rest." Ronin presented the logic like a gold-wrapped box tied with a bow. Justifiably, because it was double-pronged solution.

Maybe it was safe enough. Maybe it would help him. Whatever we were doing wasn't going to work much longer.

"Go get it. I'm going to talk to him."

I scrubbed and grabbed a juice bag. The OR stank of shit, flesh, blood, and rubbing alcohol.

Caden glanced up from his work long enough to see me. His eyes were so bloodshot the irises were lighter than the sclerae. He didn't say anything. Didn't crack a joke or ask me if I had a shot.

I pushed the straw into the bag and held it up. He nodded, keeping his fingers in his instruments. Getting the straw under his mask, I looked down. The man's ribs were spread open, and his lungs inflated and deflated. Blood bubbled in a line across one lung. The nurse cleaned the area, and I looked at her.

Without a word, she told me she was concerned.

When the juice was empty, I took it away.

"How are you holding up?" I asked him.

He nodded.

"You're not talking?"

"Clamp this here," he said to the nurse. His voice came through as a sandpaper husk.

"You should have started hallucinating."

"Just aural," he said. "Shit!"

Blood spurted everywhere. People appeared around the table, orders were shouted, and I was in the way. I backed out the door.

DAY FIVE
06:45:00

IF CADEN KNEW how often I checked on him, he'd think I was in love with him. Which I wasn't.

Not yet.

But as the days had worn on, my efforts to keep the simple, sweet fantasies from my mind were failing. They involved the days after the offensive. Meeting in the chow hall. Sitting together. Him across from me, then next to me, his boot pressed against mine under the table.

I was in the middle of one such fantasy when I saw him outside the OR for the first time in five days. He sat by a bed in recovery, talking to a soldier with an exposed chest bandage. It shouldn't have mattered who the patient was, and I wasn't kidding myself into thinking I'd have checked on any other surgeon's follow-up. But I took a look at the chart associated with the bed.

Corporal Jaskowitz. Chest wound.

What was Caden telling him?

I had never been a boy-crazy giggler. I had gone from fifth grade to full black-wearing, Nietzsche-quoting goth without ever having a sweet fantasy about cafeteria seating arrangements with the captain of the football team. Turning on a dime after I graduated high school, I got over my faux existential crisis and went to community college for a semester, where a doomed affair with my Psychology 101 professor opened my eyes to why I'd turned goth for those years.

My sexuality scared me.

Men scared me.

What I imagined letting them do to me had to be stuffed in a bag and thrown over the side of a bridge.

But in the CSH in Balad, I was tired and frayed. My emotions were coming apart, and the seams of my detachment were stretching.

Caden came through the holes. The sweet daydreams turned into something less sweet. He took what he wanted, pushing me into the ground, naked while he fucked me fully clothed. In the fantasies, I could have said stop and he would have. But I never did. He hurt me until I said I liked it. Then he hurt me more. He fucked my ass. He put his dick down my throat until

I choked. He held my body still by twisting it into painful knots. He tightened his grip on my throat until my consciousness narrowed into an expanding universe of pleasure.

"Major Frazier?" Dr. Ynez snapped me out of one such fantasy.

"Yeah?"

"I have a guy who needs you." He handed me a chart.

PFC. Sanchez had suffered a clean gunshot to the calf while running back from an IED explosion that had enemy sniper cover. Nothing twenty-four hours, a good hospital dressing, and a full course of antibiotics wouldn't fix. He was shaved bald, a proud Hispanic man with both his leg and his chin elevated.

I stood by him. "Private Sanchez, I'm Major Greyson Frazier. I'm a doctor."

"The nurse said you have to assess me before I can go back out."

"I do. May I sit?"

"Yeah, this gonna take long?"

I sat on the stool next to his bed. His left hand had a gold ring on the fourth finger and a dirty, bloodied piece of paper in the fist.

"It shouldn't if you're mentally fit." I indicated the paper. "What do you have there?"

"Nothing."

I held out my hand. "Then you won't mind if I see it."

I opened his hand and was surprised he let me. The paper wasn't really paper but more of a plastic sheet of film. It was a sonogram.

"Oh, that's wonderful. Congratulations."

"Don't take it." His voice was a dead serious command, and he glanced at me quickly before turning away again. "Major. Ma'am."

"I won't." I put my hands in my lap. "I'm surprised you're so eager to go back with this happening at home."

He didn't answer.

"How much longer is your deployment?"

"How much longer is yours?" He spit it out like an insult, as if asking how I liked being asked personal questions.

"Eleven months. This is my third deployment."

"Fine. Look, I'm not talking about this. I have time. Lots of time. I got two kids living on base in New Jersey, and they're fine. Just fine. Everyone's fine." His chin quivered. He bent his head right, then left, as if exercising his neck, fighting whatever emotion was overtaking him.

"How long you been here?"

"Five months, and I know you're trying to do the math in your head. I know what you think, and I don't care. This baby's not mine."

"How do you know it's not yours?"

"It's not my wife's either. Am I fit to serve or not?"

I clicked my pen and held it over my clipboard. "Let's go over a few questions, okay?"

"Fine."

The stress test was ridiculous. It was on the nose and had no cross-questions to confirm validity. It read like the US Army was covering its collective ass.

"Do you feel depressed or sad?"

"No."

"Do you have suicidal thoughts?"

"No."

"Do your legs or hands shake involuntarily?"

"No."

"Do you feel scared or startled for no reason?"

"No."

I ran down the questions, and he answered them all as if nothing about the war had gotten under his skin. He could have just gone home tomorrow and played ball with the kids, no problem. He was speaking in complete sentences that made sense. He could probably shoot straight. My job was done.

"All right." I slid the pen into its holder at the top of the clipboard. "I can't keep you from going back. But I can delay you."

"Why would you do that?"

"Because you're holding a sonogram of someone else's baby."

"This isn't your business, lady."

I raised an eyebrow.

"Major. Sorry, ma'am. This is personal."

"Keep in mind, Santa Claus didn't leave this rank in my stocking. It was earned. I got it because I know better. Now you can tell me what's going on, or I can delay your return to your unit until I'm sure you're not on a mission to right some wrong."

He pressed his head into his pillow and exhaled deeply. "It's Grady's kid."

"He's a buddy of yours?"

"Yeah. He's still there. His leg's pinned under a Jeep."

"And he's still there?"

I found it hard to believe that Corporal Thompson, a medic with a sense of duty a mile wide, had left a living man behind.

"Yes. When I tried to pull him away, his top came right off his bottom. I pulled him, and only a torso came. He was held together with like..." He couldn't find the words, but my mind filled in his spinal cord, intestines—everything must have been spilling out. Pfc. Sanchez didn't need an anatomy lesson. "He was screaming, 'Go in my pocket, go in my pocket, find my girl, find my girl.' Over and over... but the medevac was taking off, and Thompson pulled me away."

Either Grady was dead or so beyond help Thompson had had to make a hard calculation.

"He's alive," Sanchez continued. "I told him I'd come back. I swore it. But he gave me this and told me to find his wife. Tell her he loved her and the baby... I'm supposed to be the godfather. I had to run. Because the chopper was taking off. I had to leave him there. I can't hang around here while he's under the Jeep. You understand? I have to get him out."

"What happens if you go back and he didn't make it?"

"Just shut up!" He caught himself.

"It's all right."

"Please. I know you're an officer, but you really need to get me out of here."

I stood. I hated to leave him like that, but I couldn't force him to tolerate my presence, and I couldn't heal him in the few hours he had before he was sent back to his unit. I'd had enough time to assess that he needed to go home, but what then? Deny him the closure of knowing Grady had died even though he'd done his best?

I didn't know which was worse. Keeping him for a week to

recuperate, during which time he'd be convinced that every ticking minute brought his friend closer to death, or sending him back to where he'd be forced to confront the truth under the most stressful circumstances.

The fact was the choice wasn't mine. Like every other guy who wanted to go back out, he'd answered every question on the evaluation to ensure that outcome.

So, out he goes.

Jenn was at the computer station, managing piles of paperwork that would have frightened a less organized person. Her russet skin had lost some of its perfect sheen in the last few days.

"How is he?" she asked.

"Not good."

"He had to be dragged off a dead guy who was cut in two."

"That's not how he remembers it."

Jenn shook her head, and as I joined her in commiserating the misery of war, I saw Caden still sitting at Jaskowitz's bedside.

"THEY'RE STAKING POSITIONS," Colonel Brogue said as we walked across the campus to the command quarters. "We have those assholes on the ropes."

"Did they give you a timeline?"

"Of course not."

"I haven't heard choppers in a few hours."

"Hold your breath, Major. There's another push when the sun sets."

He shot me a wave and picked up his pace. I was dismissed.

DAY FIVE

13:15:00

THE OR WAS empty except for Caden and a nurse with a single patient. I went in.

"Captain," I said.

He nodded without looking up.

"We have a break," I said. "No more casualties for a few hours."

"Thank God," the nurse said.

"You look tired," Caden said to her, tying a knot with one hand and holding the thread taut.

She snipped it. "We all are."

"Go lie down," he said. "I'll close."

"No, I have it."

"Major Frazier's scrubbed."

She looked at me as if checking to see if I knew what I was doing. I didn't.

"Shoo, Lieutenant," Caden said.

I wanted to talk to him alone anyway, so I nodded to her.

She exhaled deeply. "Thank you." The doors swung as she backed out.

"Clamp," he said.

I handed it to him. "I'd check it before using it. I'm not a nurse."

"I did."

"So, after this, how about taking a load off?"

"Probably should. How you holding up? I saw you getting an earful from a Pfc. in the recovery room."

"Yeah. It was a hard story to hear. I can only imagine how hard it was to tell."

"Really?" He sounded surprised.

"Really. Why's that hard to believe?"

"I'd think you'd heard it all."

"You never hear it all."

"Little detachment goes a long way. Can you pull this back here?"

I didn't think I could, but he was waiting, so I built a quick wall between what I had to do and giving a shit about it and pulled the organ away.

"Thank you," he said, looking at me.

I turned away before my skin went pink.

He seemed rough with the bone and gristle, as if he was working on a slab of meat, but he found a sliver of metal that had barely shown up in the scan. I bit my tongue against telling him to take it easy.

"So," I started. "The aural hallucinations?"

"I've been tired before. I can tell the difference between reality and deliria."

"They saying anything fun?"

"Jumbles of words. Had it in residency too. And in the ER on 9/11. And 9/12."

"I hesitate to mention this," I said.

"She who hesitates is... something." He smiled, joking. "Go ahead, mention it. I know you want to tell me how handsome I am under pressure."

"You've looked better."

"Swab this here so I can see what I'm doing, would you?"

It was hard to look at the inside of a man's thigh, watch the blood flow through the veins. We weren't built to see the inner workings of our bodies so clearly. We were built to die under these circumstances.

"Don't think about it too hard," he said, reading my mind. He reached under a raw piece of human meat to remove a shard of metal. "That way lies madness. But you probably know all about that." *Plink*. The shrapnel dropped into a tray. He examined the scan.

"The human mind is nothing if not surprising."

"Get in here with a sponge so I can sew up the artery."

I did it.

"Thanks. Tell me what surprised you today," he said.

"You surprise me."

"Your strategy is textbook. Stroking my ego's the best way to keep me awake." He reached across the body and took his own threader. "Just keep it clean over here."

It took a second to realize he was talking about part of the leg, not my language when speaking about him.

"I'm not trying to do either. Nothing I say is going to get you to rest, and from what I can see, the last thing your ego needs is a good stroke."

His mask stretched when he smirked. "You're doing great, Greyson." He stitched the artery. "Tell me why my ego surprises you then."

"It doesn't. But earlier today I couldn't find you in here, and I thought maybe you'd finally taken a nap. But you weren't in your bunk."

"You checked my bunk?"

"Yes. Does that bother you?"

"If I knew you were coming, I would have covered the bed in rose petals."

I willed him to not look up and see how my cheeks reddened, but he defied my silent wish.

"I saw you in recovery," I continued. "You sat with a Corporal Jaskowitz for half an hour. What were you talking about?"

"I was telling him what to do when he got home. He needs to do physical therapy, and I know for a fact the VA won't tell him that."

The mask couldn't contain my involuntary laugh.

"What?" he asked.

"I thought you were, I don't know, talking to him about his emotional well-being."

"That's your job."

"I guess I'm not as surprised as I was."

"You can't separate a man's physical health from his mind's health. He goes home and doesn't fight for it, he's going to take a year and a half to get back on his feet. He's going to get frustrated and depressed. I did more for his mental health than a month of talking about his feelings."

He pulled the thread, and our eyes met over a stitched up femoral artery.

"You're right," I said.

His eyebrows went up the tiniest bit for the shortest moment of time. "You just surprised me."

"Worth it then."

He took the clamp off the artery. The stitches held.

"Let's clean this up and close. Then, since I have a few hours, I'll lie down."

"I'll alert the media."

He laughed.

DAY FIVE
15:45:00

HE STOPPED JUST outside the medical tent and squinted in the sunlight as if the blue of his eyes couldn't compete with the depth of the sky. He rocked back and forth slightly, then with more curve to the pendulum.

I grabbed him under the arm before he fell.

"I'm fine." When I tried to take away my support, he put his hand over mine. "Stay."

"I'll walk you to your bunk." We started in that direction.

"I haven't had a chance to arrange the rose petals."

"None required."

"You're too easy." He shook the fog out of his head. "Didn't mean it like that."

"I know. And you're too fucked up to do anything about it now anyway."

"Most days, I'd take that as a challenge."

"But not today."

"Definitely not today."

"Good to know your limits."

His trailer was neat, standard issue with few memories of home. The air was stale after less than a week. I laid him on the bed and took his boots off as if he was a drunk.

"Can you come get me when casualties come?"

"Someone will come, I'm sure."

"I want it to be you."

I sat on the edge of his bed and took his pulse. Ninety-five. High but not a heart attack.

"What was it you hesitated to mention?" His eyes were closed, and his voice was barely a whisper.

I had to scan my memory of the past hour to recall that I had been about to tell him about the vial Defense sent. "How much I like you."

"Like you too."

"And that you're a fool for pushing yourself so hard, but I can't help but admire it."

I got up to leave, but I didn't quite make it to the door.

"Major."

"Yes?"

"Please don't go."

"I have to." But I went back to him.

"I keep seeing their faces. Then their wounds. And the screaming. I keep hearing the screams." He turned away from the wall and held his hand out to me. "I'm too tired to try anything. All this... in my head. It's just sensory overload. But it's bad. Stay. Please."

I sat on the edge of the bed, not intending to do more than that, but he pulled me down with him. My body was strong enough to resist, but my heart was weak. After days of talking to men who never admitted a need or a weakness, Caden's raw humanity touched me. He was fearless in so many things that I hadn't expected vulnerability.

I curled into him, my shoulder blades to his chest, and let him put his arms around me. Against my back, he wept from exhaustion and pain. From tension and sorrow. I had to wipe my own eyes and swallow a hard lump of sobs.

Eventually, his body stopped shaking, and he slept. I waited until his breathing changed and his arms were dead weights before I slipped out of them. Kneeling by the bed, I touched his cheek. His tears had dried, but his black lashes were still stuck together.

"You're not cut out for this, Captain," I said softly.

Maybe no one was.

I put a blanket over him and left.

DAY FIVE
20:43:00

THE FIRST CHOPPER had come in an hour before, but we had enough doctors to take care of them. I'd kept a close eye on the time and peeked in on Caden's bunk twice. Five hours of solid sleep. He'd need another few days' worth to catch up, but he wouldn't get it. The last push into Fallujah was brutal, and they were coming faster than they could be admitted.

"Where's St. John?" Colonel Brogue shouted in triage.

"Resting," a nurse replied, getting her gloves on.

"Someone get him."

"I'll do it." I jumped up.

"Quick. We have more coming."

I ran to Caden's trailer, and when there was no answer to my knock, I went in. He was still on his back with his hands crossed over his chest. He didn't react to the light being turned on. I sat on the edge of his bed and leaned into his chest. Breathing steady. He didn't move when I took his pulse or when I let my hand linger over his before pulling away.

"Caden," I said.

No answer. He was out.

"Caden." I tapped his cheek. "Come on. Casualties."

I tapped his cheek harder. Nothing. I pinched his forearm gently, then harder.

He groaned.

"I'm sorry. They need you."

Deep suck of breath.

"Casualties," I repeated.

He swallowed.

"Okay," he said thickly, eyes clamping tight before opening.

"Let me help you."

I took his wrists and pulled him up. He was dead weight, but I managed to swing his legs over the side of the bed and get him sitting. His shoulders hunched, and his head hung.

"Wake up."

"Can't."

"I'll help you. Come on."

I pulled his arms, got him up a little, but he sat back down.

"Melatonin."

He named the hormone responsible for sleep. If his blood was flooded with it, he wouldn't be able to get up no matter how hard he tried.

"Do you want something to help you wake up?"

He dropped back until his head was against the wall. "Slap me."

"What?"

He didn't answer. His eyes closed again. I patted his cheek, but his breathing got the slow cadence of sleep again. I slapped harder.

"Adrenaline," he whispered.

He wanted me to slap him hard enough that the need to fight or run would release adrenaline, which would override the melatonin. He was using his own body like a pharmacy.

Fine. I planted my knees on either side of him. "I apologize in advance."

I slapped him hard. He grunted. I slapped him again. Deep, waking breath. The next slap was hard enough to make my hand hurt, so the next one was a backhand. That got him up. My hand was back for another.

"Stop. We're good."

"You sure?"

He rested his hands on my hips, making me realize I was straddling him. "Any more and you're going to turn me on. Oops, too late."

"A cold shower's going to cure you of two problems then."

Standing, I held my hand out to help him up. He stumbled to standing, looking around as if the idea of three-dimensional space confused him.

"Oh, man." He ran his fingers through his hair. "Okay. Let's do this."

I WAS WORRIED ABOUT HIM. On the way to the showers, he'd seemed disoriented, struggling to put together one coherent thought after another. He'd make a sharp comeback to something I said, then go silent or forget what he'd said. Waiting for him outside the showers, I called out to Ronin as he passed.

"Why you stalking the men's showers?"

"I'm waiting on a tired surgeon."

"St. John?"

"Yeah. He's had five hours but needs a week."

"They need him."

"I'm going to use the Defense stuff."

He nodded. "I'll go get it."

"Wait."

"What?"

I didn't want him to see me give the shot. He'd see how much I admired my patient's bottom, and I'd be ashamed. "Wait on my order."

He smirked. The effort to not look at my tits after getting an order from me was tearing him in two. I could see the thoughts behind his eyes like a movie. "Roger that."

He took off toward the psych office.

CADEN GOT out of the shower trailer looking cleaner and smelling better.

"Your boot's untied."

He looked down. "Huh." Surprised, he crouched and laced it up.

I crouched with him. "Caden."

"Major."

"This isn't giving me confidence that you should be in an operating room."

The *thup-thup-thup* of choppers came from the sky.

"It's an untied boot."

"I'm going to give you a shot before you go in."

"More speed?"

"Yes."

"Can you do me a favor?" he asked as we stood.

"Depends."

"Go in my trailer. In my footlocker's a set of keys with a rabbit's foot. It's right on top. Take the rabbit's foot off and put it in your pocket."

"For what?"

"For you. You need it."

"What do I need a rabbit's foot for?"

"It's a useless talisman but might take the edge off your worry."

I put my hands on my hips. Was he being a jerk? Or was he doing something helpful and nice? I couldn't assume malice. "Thanks, I guess."

"Combination's 2259."

"See you in the scrub room."

AFTER I GAVE him the shot, I went to his bunk. I slid his footlocker from under his bed and opened it. The scent that came from it was concentrated sex. Freshly ground coffee. Wool. His clothes were neatly pressed and folded. He might have learned that in the military, but I doubted it. A man was born with this level of precision.

His keys weren't on top. They were under the first layer of army-green shirts.

A car key for a Mercedes. A house key. A metal keychain inscribed with "Never Forget 9/11." A white rabbit's foot.

I removed the furry knob and replaced the keys. Before closing the lid, I inhaled deeply and ran my hand over the shirts, pretending he was in them.

Chapter Four

DAY EIGHT

14:56:00

The battle took five weeks, but the initial offensive was over after eight days.

Caden had gone three more nonstop. No catnaps. No lie-downs. The synthetic speed did its job twice over.

When the last soldier was sewn up and the party had started in the mess hall, he was in no condition to celebrate. I found him standing shirtless over the linen hamper, scrubs balled in a fist, a marble statue of a man.

"Hey," I said. "It's over for now."

He opened his fist and let the scrubs fall into the bin. "I'm tired."

"Ya think?"

I reached for his hand so I could check his pulse. That was what I told myself. But when I took it and slid my hands to his wrist and down to his elbow in a long stroke and he lifted his arm to cup my jaw, there was no more lying.

He kissed me as if he'd been on hunger strike and our first kiss was the nourishment he'd been denying himself. As if he couldn't bear to not kiss me for another second.

Or maybe that was what I was feeling, because I clutched the back of his neck like a woman terrified of losing something. My mouth devoured him with the force of a catapult held in tension for too long yet sprung too fast. My hands released his neck and ran over the crests and valleys of his body. He pushed me against the table and pressed his fingers between my legs. The fabric was damp and hot.

"Fuck," he growled between his teeth before planting his mouth on mine again.

I wrapped my legs around his waist, and he pushed his erection against me. Through three layers of army-issue garments, he was hot and hard, pushing against my pussy as if he could disintegrate everything between us. He jerked his hips to stimulate my clit, and I shifted mine to rub against the length of him.

"Yes," I groaned. "That's good."

He jerked again, and I shifted again, until we fell into such a hard rhythm we couldn't kiss anymore. We rubbed together, hard against hot, watching each other's faces, panting against the other's lips.

His eyes scrunched, and his jaw clenched. He planted his elbows behind my shoulders and held my head.

"Close, I'm—" I gasped.

He ground against me harder. Faster. "Yes."

The orgasm went on and on—a gradual release of pressure through the tiniest hole. Even as he thrust his cock against me, the incidental stimulation wasn't ever enough all at once. It was cumulative, and I broke slowly, over and over, spilling my climax into tears and long, hitching sobs as he had his own orgasm, exhaling into my neck.

My tears didn't stop. I wept onto his skin, shaking under him. The stories I'd heard. The pain I'd seen. Everything. The brain-injured bodies being shipped home. I'd watched so much suffering and bottled it away. Caden shattered it, then kissed the tears off my cheeks.

He reached for a towel and wiped his semen off the front of my uniform as I wept. His dick had come free of the drawstring scrubs. He wiped off his belly, redid the string, and reached over me for a new shirt.

I tried to get up, but that only drove me into his arms. God, I wanted him.

"Sleep with me," he said.

"Like last time?"

"No. This time, I'm going to try to fuck you, and you're going to let me."

MY TRAILER WAS NICER, but we went to his without discussion. The entire camp was relaxing with music and alcohol, but when he closed the door, we were in our own world. He peeled off his shirt and dropped his scrubs, stepping out of his underwear in one move.

The floodlights came through a crack in the blinds, casting his cock's shadow over his leg. I unbuttoned my shirt, and he got on his knees before me, undoing the metal belt buckle.

"You hungry?" He slid the belt through the metal clasp.

"No."

"Thirsty?" Button and zipper undone, he kissed the panties under it.

"I'm all right."

"I have bottled water for later."

"How much later can you stay awake?"

He slid my pants down as I got my shirt off.

"I can stay awake long enough to come in you. Come on you. Come with you." He looked up at me and pulled my panties down. "I can stay awake long enough to suck you, finger you, fuck you." His hands ran down my legs to get my underwear off. When he got to my feet, he pushed them apart. "As long as you can stay awake tonight." Watching my face, he ran his fingers from deep in the crack of my ass, to my wet pussy, to the throbbing nub at the other side. "That's how long you'll be coming."

He slid two fingers inside me. "Look at me."

I did. Even from waist level, he was in charge.

"Birth control," he said.

"I'm on it."

He spread the lips apart and laid his fluttering tongue against my exposed clit. My knees turned to jelly, and I nearly fell over. He stood and whipped the chair from behind the desk, guiding me into it.

"These past eight days," he said, lifting one of my legs over an arm of the chair. "Eight days of hell. You made them bearable." He draped the other leg over the other arm, until my wet pussy was fully exposed to him. The way he looked at it was more arousing than my previous lovers' touches. "I trusted you with myself, and you did right by me." He was on his knees again, a hand on the inside of each thigh. "Thank you."

"You could just write me a note."

"I might still," He kissed my knee and all the way up to the center. "But I've wanted you since the minute I saw you." He gave my clit a little suck. "You came off the Chinook like you could conquer the Republican Army all by yourself." Another suck, and I put my fingers in his hair. "So fucking sexy." He took my hands away and laid them on my knees. "All I wanted to do was conquer you."

He held my hands and knees together and went to work with his tongue. Sucking and licking until I was close, then stopping to circle my entrance to bring the sensations there. Back up to my clit, over and over.

"Let me come," I gasped, looking down at him. "Don't stop this time."

"You don't rank me here."

"What do you want?"

"Say please."

"Please."

He brought me close again, then stopped to run his tongue over my opening again.

"Please, Caden."

"You're too sexy when you're close." He sucked me gently. Stopped.

"No! God, please let me come. Please. I'm begging."

"I like that."

"Please," I whispered.

He ran his tongue along me and put his lips over my clit, locking on it with a hard suck that he continued while flicking his tongue against the raw, needy flesh.

The climax was blinding. My body pulsed, pushed, throbbed with him.

His lips were on mine, and I tasted myself in his mouth. He lifted me onto the bed. I was overstimulated, still shaking when he put the head of his cock against me and pushed. I wasn't big enough for him, but I was so slick he got in, stretching me to pain I didn't find unpleasant.

Holding my hands over my head, he kissed me, fucked me, owned me. When I came again, he drove harder and deeper, as if he wanted to bury himself inside me, and the pain grounded me and drove me over the edge at the same time.

"Take it," he gasped his last command.

He came in a twist of muscle, gripping tight, white-knuckled, red in the face, then releasing like a shattered glass in an explosion of potential energy gone kinetic and dissolving into sweat and gulped breaths.

"Wow," he said, kissing my collarbone, still inside me.

"Wow is right." I held his cheeks while he caught his breath.

"Wow."

"Right. Yes..."

"That was a great start."

LATE IN THE NIGHT, pleasantly sore and sticky where it counted, I drifted off to sleep while he stroked my shoulder in a way that was both casual and intentional.

"Why aren't you sleeping?" I asked with the last of my waking energy.

"I fell asleep first last time."

"Didn't count."

"I like looking at you."

"Mm."

He kissed my shoulder. I hoped he didn't want to fuck again. I was tired, and I was sure that if he wanted to, he'd need thirty seconds to make me want him again.

"All the time," he continued. "You're hard to not look at. When you're working with some jarhead who would rather be dead than talking to a psychiatrist, the way you listen? Even if he's got his back turned to you or he's telling you to fuck off? Like there's no one else in the world but that one guy? You're stunning. If you ever looked at me like that, I'd tell you everything."

I wanted to say, "Tell me everything right now." But my lips wouldn't form the words, and my lungs could only breathe in the rhythms of slumber.

Part Two

Chapter Five

The week after the first surge, the doctors went on doctoring while the surgeons were put on rest. Casualties came in at a manageable rate for the normal rotation, which I no longer oversaw.

After our first night together, Caden had slept for twenty-four hours. Most of the surgeons had. He owned me the two nights after that. Rotation last night. And tonight? If it was up to me, I'd be his again tonight.

The army was a huge net of people with tight knots of community. The way Ronin and I had found each other from basic, to Walter Reed, back around again to a common assignment in Iraq wasn't unheard of. But Caden? He wasn't part of the net. He'd sought out a commission during a time of war. As soon as his obligation was done, he could, and would, leave to pick up his life where he'd left it.

Like a soldier who'd witnessed the unthinkable, I tried not to think about it.

"Captain Fobbit!" Sergeant "Little Red" Ryder cried from across the dusty field, a football crooked behind his shoulder.

Caden, the fobbit in question, held his arm out to indicate he was open. Ryder released the ball across the sky like a drill, cutting the blue only to have it enfold around its wake. Caden picked the ball out of the air but was tackled by Ronin and Pfc. "Salt Mine" Trona. They slapped his back when they got off him. I held my hand out to help him up.

"What's with that Ronin guy?" He grabbed my wrist so I could pull him up. "He was all over you. He think you're Jerry Rice or something?"

"Ryder usually throws to me."

He snapped the ball back to Ryder without an answer, and we headed for the line of scrimmage.

"You shouldn't let them call you fobbit," I said. "It's not nice."

"How's that?"

"Means you never go outside the wires. Means you don't know shit."

"Maybe I don't." He smirked as if he really believed he lacked a necessary piece of knowledge about anything important.

Sergeant Ryder called out the play numbers, and we fell back. This time, I got the jump on my coverage, and the ball landed right in my hands. Ronin got to me, knocking me three feet out of a run in an attempted tackle, but I wouldn't go down. He reached around me, trying to strip the ball away.

I cried, "Foul, foul," but we were both laughing and fighting to the death as I pushed toward the Humvee tire marking the end zone.

Ronin's weight was suddenly off me, and I ran for the line, where I spiked the ball into the sand.

My victory was short-lived. Caden was on top of Ronin with his knee in his back, pushing his face into the ground while Ryder and Trona were arriving to pull Caden off.

"You don't touch her like that, you hear me?"

Ronin was on his feet. "What is your fucking problem?"

"Watch your goddamn hands."

Ronin held up his palms. "I don't know what the fuck is going on here..."

"Like fuck you don't," Caden said.

Trona picked up the ball and tossed it to Ryder.

"All right, whatever. Fuck this." Ronin slapped the dirt off his hands and walked away.

Ryder and Trona passed the ball between them. Game over.

"What was that about?" I asked Caden.

"What's going on with him and you?"

"Football."

Of course, I knew what he meant. And yes, my answer was evasive. But he was acting like a child, and children aren't owed explanations for adult decisions.

"Why are you lying?"

I got right in his beautiful fucking face. "Because you're being an asshole."

I stormed off.

THAT NIGHT, in chow hall, he sat with the other surgeons, and I sat with Ronin. It was as if, after the bell, we'd gone back to our respective corners of the ring without even knowing we'd been boxing.

How did I know he was watching me? How did I know every time he glanced my way as if he happened to be looking out the window?

I was watching him as well.

"I got orders to go to Abu Ghraib," Ronin said.

"Are you even allowed to tell me that?"

"If I did, then I am."

I pushed corn around my plate, trying to pretend Caden wasn't there. My will was weak. When I lifted the fork to my mouth, our eyes met across the room, and he looked away.

"Well, I guess your work here is done," I said.

"The army's work."

"Yeah."

Caden got up with his tray. Why did that tie my heart into a knot? The surprise of seeing him get up? The broken string of our mutually denied gaze?

"Before I go, I want to make you an offer."

"That's intriguing." Not as intriguing as Caden leaving his tray on the pile and walking out of chow hall with one of the guys on the Australian surgery team, chatting and laughing over who even knew what. Livers and spleens.

He had no business laughing over internal organs when I felt so crappy about fighting with him.

"I've known you since the beginning," Ronin said. "Since you broke your wrist in basic."

"And you pushed me over the wall."

"Any other guy would have laid you down gently and called for help. I made sure you finished the course."

I nodded. "You did the right thing."

"I know. Because you and me? We understand each other. I need to not be tied down. You need to be pushed."

"And you have an offer to push me?"

"The offer has two parts. You can take one without the other."

"I'm listening."

"Part one. I'm going to Abu Ghraib in advance of a different kind of battle. A psychological one. We're going to be fighting the enemy using a new weapon: their own culture."

"How?"

"I can't say, obviously, but it's within the Geneva Convention protocols. It's a war of the mind. No bloodshed. No death. None of this shit." He checked to make sure no one was in earshot, then leaned forward. "You have a way with talking to shell-shocked men. You get it. And you speak Arabic. I want to talk to my command about loaning you out from your unit. Now this is up to you, and it's totally voluntary. It's a unicorn. Cherish the moment. You have a *choice* in the matter."

My ambition muscled out my patience and sense. I was interested before even hearing the details. "What's the second part?"

"It's optional."

"Okay."

"You come to Abu Ghraib *with* me."

"*With?*"

"Here it is. Straight out. Friends with benefits has been great, but I'd like to spend more time with you."

My ambition sat down, crossed her legs and arms, and scowled. "Christ, Ronin. Is this a unicorn too?"

"I'm not looking for a long-term commitment or anything big, but—"

"But I won't sleep with you in Balad, so you want to push me because I need to be pushed?"

A smile stretched across his face. "You get me." When I rolled my eyes, he took my hand. "In the past week, I realized I like you more than I thought. I know, I'm being a typical male, but I'm not lying. I want you, and if that means cornering you into a new job, I'll do it."

"You put the brutal in brutally honest, did you know that?"

I pulled my hand away, but it was too late. Caden had come back into the room. Our eyes met, and he was not smiling. I could hardly think sandwiched between these two men. One of them had to go away, and it wasn't Caden.

"Give me a day," I said to Ronin, picking up my tray. I wanted to get out of there before I suffocated. I needed to consider the half of his offer that wasn't wrapped in carnal payoffs.

"You want to put me second in line after Captain Fobbit over there, that's your call. He's going to put you in a cage and throw away the key."

The way he thought he knew me was exhausting enough. He couldn't have a clue about Caden.

"You're wrong."

"Give it time. He will."

"No, I mean I'm not putting you second in line. There is no line."

I put my tray on the pile and went to Caden. A string between us pulled taut enough to trip anyone that crossed between. A string of my intentions. My forward motion and his patience as I walked in his direction, my determination to tell him exactly how I felt even as I defined my feelings to myself.

I didn't owe him an explanation about Ronin or any other lover. I could do whatever I wanted with my body, and if he'd expected some kind of fidelity, he should have brought it up. I didn't owe him my time or my attention.

I owed him none of those things, but I wanted him to have them. My fidelity. My time. My attention, my honesty and respect—all given as gifts whether he wanted them or not.

My mother told me the moment a person falls in love is often quiet. It often comes in the night, or when you're paying attention to something else, but it's always in the rearview. You don't meet love in the moment. It's not an ambush. Someone chips away at the stone façade around it, breaching your fortifications, crippling your defenses, and the moment you fall in love is the moment you realize what you've built the wall around was love. You fall in love with your conqueror.

I didn't love him.

Not yet. But bit by bit, he was chipping away at my battlements.

Walking toward him, his face softening as mine hardened, I

knew I could love him. One day, I'd look in my rearview and see what had been there all along.

I was two steps away. I could see the hair on his face and the set of his jaw. Another step and I could whisper to him. I still didn't know what I would say or which part of love's barricades I'd start with. I didn't know if I'd open with reassurance or a challenge, but I was sure, when I got there, I'd say the right thing.

"Hear ye! Hear ye!" Lieutenant Farrow stood on a chair with his arms wide, a clipboard in one hand.

Caden and I were eyelocked with a few feet between us, stock still at the first "hear ye."

"Gather 'round, soldiers and citizens, while I tell you a statistical tale of eight days in hell."

Caden took the last two steps in my direction, closing the gap completely, but we were now surrounded by the entire camp.

"The medical team in the combat support hospital saw 231 casualties for 208 hours." He read the team's achievements like a carnival barker. "Not one of three operating rooms was empty for eight days."

"I need to know," Caden said softly. "What's going on with him?"

"Why do you need to know?"

His eyes lit up like the end of a short fuse, getting brighter when ignited with a little anger.

Farrow went on in the background. "Brogue's on the other side of the wire, so it falls on yours truly—"

"I don't want to share you."

"You're not sharing me."

"—and so! In the spirit of giving out trophies before the game's even done—"

"I hope you mean that the same way I do, Greyson. Because I don't just mean your body. I don't want to share your time or your heart or your happy fucking thoughts."

"—most likely to have a juice box handy... Lieutenant Keston! Come up—"

"Nobody owns me, Caden. Those things are given freely or not at all."

"Give them to me then."

He was getting them, but he wasn't entitled. His tone made my hair stand on end and my palms sweat. I didn't know whether to fuck him or run away.

"You can't demand any of that."

Behind him, Lt. Keston received a bedpan filled with foil juice bags. She thanked the Academy.

"Give me everything or nothing. If it's no, just say so now. Is it no?"

I felt cornered. Caught in the middle of a tunnel as the walls shook from an oncoming train.

"—likely to be mistaken for a medical machine—"

"Yes or no?"

"Maybe."

"This game you're playing isn't a game to me. You can hurt me."

Again, I was caught. This time between reassuring him and telling him I wouldn't be emotionally blackmailed. Between admiring his willingness to be vulnerable and disdaining his manipulations. All and/or/but nothing.

"—Doctor Caden Has-A-Word-Missing-On-His-Tape John—"

All eyes were on us. Farrow held up a rubber chicken, waving Caden over while everyone applauded. He curled his mouth into a smirk. Caden took a deep breath and stepped toward the guy holding the rubber chicken.

That was when the earth shook.

"Mortar fire!" someone shouted.

A dozen doctors, nurses, and medics dropped everything and ran for the door, including Caden.

He turned for a half second to address me. "We'll talk later."

He didn't wait for me to agree but ran behind the last nurse. I was left with a newly buzzing chow hall and a list of questions.

I went outside, hearing the click of debris falling on rooftops. The mortar had fallen halfway between the chow hall and the airstrip. One of the supply sheds was on fire. The medical teams mobilized, and what looked like chaos of running and shouting was actually a well-rehearsed effort to get the wounded into the hospital.

My job was to stay out of the way until everyone was moved. Hoses came out. Fires were doused. The smoke in the air cleared. I went to the hospital to see if there was anything I could do.

Jenn was setting up an IV line. Her hands shook.

"That was scary," she said when she was out of the patient's earshot. "I was practically on top of it, but I had to pee... so..." Her eyes filled up as she put on a latex glove. "I walked over to the latrine."

I squeezed her biceps. "You're in psychological shock."

"I'm fine." She took off the glove.

"You're shaking."

"They need me." She pinched her fingers together to put the glove back on.

"What's with the glove?"

She froze, looking at it as if she didn't know why it hung from her fingertips like a jellyfish.

"Jenn, you can't hook up any more lines until you pull it together."

"Oh, my God."

"'Oh, my God' what?"

"I don't remember putting any lines in."

The hit had traumatized her, even if temporarily.

"Let's double check what you did."

We checked the IVs and stents. She'd done it all perfectly, as if autopilot had worked even if the plane was about to crash.

"I'm not doing this anymore," she said. "Last deployment."

It was the first time she'd ever said that.

While she reported to her superior, I peeked into the OR. Dr. Ynez worked on a casualty from the mortar attack. No Caden. I checked for him in recovery. Not there either. He could have been anywhere. I couldn't ask without someone wondering why I cared where he was. Or worse, they wouldn't ask.

"Greyson?" Jenn said, coming back from her superior.

"Yeah, hey. What did Yvonne say?"

"Sent me back to quarters."

I walked her to the trailers. She was still shaky but managed to brush her teeth and carry on a conversation.

"You might not be able to sleep tonight," I said.

"I don't *feel* traumatized." She spit into the sink.

"Your brain doesn't care how you feel."

"Fucking brain." She looked at herself closely in the mirror. "I swear to God, what this war does to people."

"Any war."

"Any. All. I just wanted to go to college. I feel like I'm ruining the same brain I was trying to educate."

I hugged her. "You'll be okay."

She patted my back and pulled away. "We'll see."

"We will. Come on. I'll tuck you in."

JENN WAS SAFELY IN BED. I'd check on her in the morning. I should have gone to bed too. The mortar area was taped off. The casualties had been treated and assessed. There was nothing left for me to do. But I was energized. Hyper. Activated.

I wanted to see Caden. I told myself I wanted to make sure he was okay, but the fact was I wanted him to tell me I was okay.

His trailer was dark, and he didn't come to the door when I knocked. He wasn't in the chow hall. Or the hospital.

"Hey," I said to a doctor in recovery.

She leaned over a patient who had gauze over his eyes. With her blond hair tied into a neat ponytail, I didn't recognize her.

"Hi." She smiled.

I held out my hand. "I'm Major Greyson."

She shook it. "Ferguson. I'm stationed at the airfield."

"Oh, nice to meet you."

Airfield surgeons went into combat with the medevac teams. Dr. Ferguson had vibrant skin and clear eyes. She didn't look like a woman who went to the front lines in a Blackhawk, but that assumption said more about me than her.

"I have an eye specialty, and they traded me," she said.

"Traded?"

"For a general surgeon, oddly, not a field doc. I was going to rush back, but they'd already left on a nine-line with him. That won't go over well."

General surgeons were too valuable to go past the wire.

"Did his name happen to be Captain St. John?"

"Yeah. Hard name to forget. He jumped right in. Volunteered like that." She snapped her fingers.

The medevacs did not fuck around with time. Caden must have jumped on the truck to the airfield, told them he was a doctor, and taken off.

Caden outside the wire. Everything could go wrong. What was he thinking?

He wanted to own me, but he didn't even know me. He didn't know I had brother in Afghanistan or that my father had been eaten alive every day by regret and guilt even as he gave more and more years in service. He hadn't grown up with stories of blood and gore, rage and impotence. I had. The fact that I'd chosen to serve in a war zone didn't mean I fetishized battle. It meant I went in with my eyes open.

I wished I'd had time to open his eyes, and when he got back, I was making it my job to put away all our power games and make sure he didn't deploy again. He was going to hear about my father's night terrors, my brother's suicide attempt, my grandfather's guilt. Eight days of treating soldiers who had been blown to bits was going to seem like a cakewalk.

Caden was going home after this deployment if I had to scare the shit out of him.

I COULDN'T MILL around the airfield like a lost lamb. I kept my eyes on the dark sky and my ears open for approaching birds. I wasn't privy to what was happening, whether they'd landed under fire or at all. Nothing.

I should have told him the truth right away, without backpedaling or soft-shoeing. I was his. Completely. Unabashedly. Unreservedly. Instead of enforcing my will, I should have opened myself with the same nakedness he had.

My desk was piled with paperwork. Since I wasn't going to sleep until I knew Caden was all right, and my office was close enough to the hospital to hear when they brought in casualties, I figured I'd do it.

When I pulled out my chair, I found a small manila envelope with my name on the front. I undid the string, and a dirty, blood-streaked sonogram fell into my hand. I shook it, and a folded piece of paper came out. A note.

Pfc Sanchez came in again. Head trauma.
Said to give this to the psychiatrist.
He didn't make it.

NO ONE HAD DIED on Balad Base unless they had severe brain trauma. We didn't have the capacity to treat it. We could only send them to Baghdad as quickly as possible. For Sanchez, that obviously hadn't been quick enough. Wife and two kids. Damn. Just damn.

What had he said his buddy's name was? Grady? First name or last? I'd find his wife and tell the story if she wanted to hear it.

I put the sonogram and the note back into the envelope before I started on the paperwork.

"IT WAS COLONEL BROGUE OUT THERE."

In the dead quiet of the midnight hour, the staff nurse's voice carried through the wall. Brogue had wanted to get off base, and it sounded as if he'd done just that. I stopped what I was doing as a less-clear voice mumbled something.

"Little bird got them after the area was secured. All the casualties went to Baghdad. We're clear."

I bolted up from my chair and got my jacket.

I CAUGHT a ride to the airfield and waited in the little kitchen, trying to stay out of the way, asking what I could and overhearing the rest.

From what I could glean, Caden's Blackhawk had landed under fire, which pilots aren't supposed to do until they do it, then they're responsible. With a full bird colonel on the ground, it wasn't surprising they'd taken the risk, but there wasn't supposed to be human gold in the form of a trauma surgeon on the chopper either.

They'd taken fire. Other casualties. Local civilians had gotten involved. They'd lifted out with the wounded when they knew a little bird was coming for Caden and the minor injuries.

The lighter *thups* of the smaller helicopter came out of the pale morning sky, and I went outside. With the sun kissing the horizon, the ground was still dark, and the airfield floodlights were necessary. The passengers were shadows in the glass as it landed. I held my jacket tightly around me, approaching into the wind of the rotors to see him, ready to tell him everything, reassure him, give myself to him, scare him out of this life.

He got out of the helicopter after the last of the passengers as the pilot slowed the whirr of the rotor. The front of this shirt and pants were solid black, as if he'd lain in a puddle of ink.

I ran to him. That particular shade of black was the result of the floodlights hitting the deep red of blood.

He didn't stop. He looked straight ahead, passing me by as if he didn't see me.

"Caden!"

He got in the back seat of the Jeep, where the driver waited for him. I looked in the window. He was staring straight ahead, in a fugue state, seeing nothing.

What the hell had happened out there?

I CAUGHT a ride behind him and ran to his trailer right out of the seat.

His door wasn't closed all the way. I knocked. No answer. Knocked again.

"Caden," I said.

I respected his privacy up to a point, and I'd reached it. Pushing the door, I stepped into the dark room. A band of morning sunlight fell into the corner, catching his bowed, blood-soaked figure. I shut the door, making sure it clicked closed. No one needed to see him sitting in the corner with his arms around his knees.

Crouching in front of him, I laid my hands on his arms and looked into his face. He kept staring into the middle distance.

"Caden."

With barely any pressure on his arms, they dropped to his sides as if he were dead. Paresis. I put my fingers to his neck. Warm life pulsed there. I caressed his face with that hand, but he didn't respond.

"I'm going to get someone in here to bring you to the hospital."

"No." His voice was low and flat, and hearing it cut open my worry enough to let out my sorrow.

I didn't know what had happened, but it had broken him. This man who had worked eight days with no more than a short rest, who had let his sense of duty guide him to do the impossible, who had touched me with his vulnerability and strength... they'd broken him.

Oh sure, they'd get him functioning again, because they needed him, but he'd be thrown away because only the weak were broken by war, and the US military had no room for the weak.

"You're not weak," I said more to myself than him. "Do you hear me?" He gave no indication that he did or didn't, but he'd heard me suggest moving him to the hospital, so I continued. "You didn't have to prove anything to me. You owned me from the moment I saw you, and you never, ever shared me. Do you understand?"

He swallowed.

"Fuck them," I said more to myself than him, standing.

The army had broken him. The army was going to fix him.

I stormed out into the morning sun. I got thirty feet away. The Humvee tire we'd used as an end zone was at the other side of the field, another thirty feet away. My mind was strategizing who to tap for help and where they were when the mortar hit.

The earth shook, and with a sharp pain in my ears, everything went silent. When I landed on my back, I couldn't even hear the breath exit my lungs, but I felt it with the agony in my chest.

The silence was more disorienting than the rain of rocks and shrapnel.

I got my feet under me. Dizzy. Planting my feet. Breathing soundlessly with a sharp pain in my chest. I looked down at myself. I was covered in blood. When I looked back up, I realized I'd been turned around. Caden stood at his door, awakened by the blast, his blood-soaked shirt mirroring mine, crying out without a sound.

The ground rotated under me.

I was falling.

I would hit the dirt at the acceleration of gravity.

I couldn't break my fall, but I didn't need to.

A man was under me, catching me, holding me in his arms as he ran.

Deaf but not blind, I could only see the blue sky. The black smoke from the mortar bounded my peripheral vision on one side.

When he looked down at me for a second, he wasn't broken anymore. The eternal sky was captured in his eyes, deadly and comforting, alive with purpose.

I REMEMBERED cool sheets under my head.

I remembered a drowning feeling.

I remembered bright light through the fog of my vision and choking on a tube.

I remembered the blood cooling on my skin when they cut off my clothes.

I remembered his eyes set over the rectangle of a surgical mask, cutting through the fog with unguarded concern and utter confidence.

I could never forget the love in them.

Chapter Six

A single shard of metal had missed my heart by two millimeters.

"There's more ways to miss a heart than hit it," Caden said from beside my bed.

He'd used his R&R days to fly into Baghdad after me. The incision was small. I could have recuperated in Balad, but Caden had stepped in, making sure I was in the best-equipped hospital whether I needed it or not.

"I prefer to think of myself as lucky."

"Preference noted. They're sending you back to the CSH."

He was making an assumption that I was going back to Balad based on the fact that I was going back into the field. I was indeed going back into the field—but not to the CSH.

"What happened out there?" I asked. "Outside the wire?"

He shrugged and looked away. "The usual intense shit."

"I saw Brogue." My CO was down the hall with another injury so close to deadly it confirmed the existence of luck for me—and the existence of statistical probability of survival for Caden's patients.

Brogue being down the hall had its benefits. I'd wheeled down there and checked on him. He was going home, but he was still the commanding officer of the First Medical Brigade. He could task me out of my unit up to Abu Ghraib to work with Army Intelligence for a while.

He'd agreed it was an opportunity to go from a specialty no one respected to something where I could move up, make a difference, release myself from the constraints of a unit for a while and decide how I wanted to work. He'd do the paperwork as soon as he could sit up in his goddamned bed.

If I went through with it, I wasn't going back to the support hospital with Caden.

"He said you saved his life and a few others," I continued. "He's recommended you for a commendation."

"I get a nice pat on the back whenever I do my job." He squeezed my hand and ran his finger along my forearm with a touch that was uniquely his.

"Why did you go out?" I asked. "There are field surgeons who could have gone."

"You asked me this, Greyson."

"And you deflected, which I let you do because I was post-op."

Four fingertips went back down my forearm with a tenderness that could only be described as worshipful. "You don't let stuff go, do you?"

"Nope."

"I want to be with you. Do you want to be with me?"

"Yes. More than anything."

"And if we are a couple, this is what I can expect? You to lock onto things?"

I didn't want to turn him off, but I wouldn't lie to him either. "Yep. But I'm also patient. I won't forget, but I'll let you tell me things in your own time."

He stared at the way his thumb stroked the scars on my wrist. "I went out to prove that I could."

That wasn't news. I could have told him that. But having him say it so plainly was unexpected and earth-shattering and a chest-spreader, exposing my heart to his attention.

"You didn't need to do that."

"I did. Not for you. For me. And maybe you a little. I knew you'd say it didn't matter, but I didn't want to look in your eyes in ten years and wonder if you ever thought you could do better."

Ten years?

I was crazy about him. Infatuated. I wanted nothing more than to continue this relationship for all it was worth. Bleed him dry emotionally. Suck him to the bare, delicious, raw core.

But ten years? How was that even possible?

"Caden."

"Greyson?"

So impossibly blue, his eyes were holes to the sky.

"I can't do better," I said.

"Well, I know that."

We smiled, and I looked away. "But you're not staying in the military, and this is my life."

"I do catch movies sometimes. Guy's off on deployment and calls his woman from base. She's always in the kitchen of some suburban house, holding the phone with both hands because she loves him. We can just switch it. You call me. I'll hold the phone with both hands."

"In a suburban house?"

"Probably not. That a deal-breaker?"

"No. Not that."

He didn't ask me what the deal-breaker was. Either he didn't want to know, or he was aware of what I didn't yet know.

There were no deal-breakers.

"We don't have to decide now," he said.

"How much longer do you have here?" I shook my head. He had almost a year *here* in Iraq, but that wasn't what I meant. "In Baghdad?"

"I'm on call tomorrow morning. We're still trying to retake Fallujah, you know. But I'll try to come back to get you."

"That's not necessary."

"I know. But I worked it out with my CO and some of the other guys. We switched stuff around. We're fine until the next offensive. And if they need me, you just have to come back without an escort."

"My feminine heart wouldn't stand it, sir. Imagine what could happen?"

He put his hand on my face and kissed me. "I pity the poor slob who tries to keep you from me."

"Me too."

We kissed again.

"You're tired." He told me that as if he knew me better than I knew myself, and though it seemed too soon for that to be possible, he was right.

"I can't wait to be at a hundred percent again."

Caden pressed the button that lowered the bed to a sleeping position. "You at a hundred percent is what I want." He stroked my face. "Close your eyes."

They wanted nothing more than to shut so I could fully feel his touch slide over my skin.

"Once you're at a hundred percent," he whispered, "I'm going to fuck you down to twenty. When your arms are limp and you've come so many times you think you can't come again, you're going to curl up next to me to try to sleep. I won't let you. I'll fuck you down to ten percent. I'm going to leave you at five before I let you sleep." I opened my eyes halfway, but he closed them with a brush of his hands. "Just sleep."

"Stay."

"I brought paperwork. I'll be right here, cursing it."

"Mmm."

My arms and legs got heavy and my mind drifted away until I felt as if I had no body at all except for where Caden touched me and where a piece of metal had sliced a thin, throbbing hole in my chest.

CADEN CAME BACK for a day when I was well enough to leave the hospital. We went to a nearby teashop filled with enough American servicemen that it was all right to have an unmarried woman and man at the same table. He left on the next Phrog out.

"I wish I could drive," he said absently as the rotors *thupped*.

"It's ten times more dangerous."

"Yeah."

I knew that look, and his "yeah" was more than a simple agreement over the danger of on-road travel. "Caden?"

"Major?"

"Are you afraid to fly?"

"No." He waved away his answer. "Not in a plane. Not a 'flight,' with tickets and an airport. But those damn helicopters. They have a way of dropping out of the sky."

"I think they more spin than drop."

He smiled, and I was disarmed. I wanted to offer him the same openness he'd given me.

"Also," I said, "me too. These things terrify me. I white-knuckle it the whole way."

His eyebrows went up. I was glad I still had the ability to surprise him.

"The enormity of falling," I continued. "Feeling the space around me and floating in it?" I shivered. "I'd almost rather risk an IED."

"Good thing we don't get to make that call."

"Good thing."

He held my hand, focusing on where our bodies knotted.

"There's this jumper picture from 9/11," he said. "A couple holding hands on the way down."

I'd seen it, and I had to consider for a moment that it meant something for him it didn't mean for me. Everything from that day would have layers of meaning for him.

"You think it was your parents?"

"No. It's not. But I like to think that her last action was to refuse his hand. Tell him no."

"Do you want me to tell you no?"

"I want to never give you a reason to."

"I'M NOT GOING HOME," I said into the hospital phone. Jenn was on the other side of the line. I had an envelope stamped with the US Army seal crunched in my hand.

"Why not?"

"The incision was nothing. It was clean."

"You lost a ton of blood."

"I have it back. I'm replenished like a vampire."

"Well, it'll be nice to have you around."

I didn't think it would be hard to tell her, but I had to take a second to rework what I intended to say. "I'm not staying. Not for long. I got tasked out to Defense."

"Where?"

"I'm heading up to ABG."

My paperwork had gone through. Brogue was laid up and on his way home but had signed the recommendation. The approval had come in the envelope my palm was sweating on.

"Abu Ghraib? Why? For what?"

"I can't—"

"It's Ronin."

"It's Ronin," I confirmed.

"Okay, I'm saying this once, then you do what you want, okay?"

"This should be good."

"It will be. Write it down."

I laughed silently so she couldn't hear me, but I had the feeling I wouldn't need to write it down. "Go ahead."

"You do not have the moral vacancy required to work with the DoD."

"The project conforms to the Geneva Convention."

"Okay, if he has to say that, then that's a problem. And have you asked yourself what he needs you for?"

I didn't, and wouldn't, mention the second part of Ronin's offer, but my pause while I decided that was enough of an opening for Jenn to jump in.

"The medical degree," she said. "You can script and dispense."

"It's my job."

"I don't like it. It bothers me."

"You're just going to miss me."

"Yeah. That too."

Chapter Seven

Caden wasn't able to come to Baghdad to escort me back to the CSH. Despite his commission, he was and always would be a civilian—with a civilian's confidence in his own agency. He'd always think he could make decisions, work around the rules while staying in the lines, negotiate with his superiors, charm his way through a narrow opening in his options.

On the Chinook, with my knuckles pale caps over where my fingers and my hand joined, I wondered how he would tolerate my career. Military wives had to submit to a host of indignities, starting with a loss of control over where they lived and ending with a loss of control over parenting. Their husbands were married to the military first. How would Caden manage always playing second to the army, especially when, after two deployments, he still didn't understand how little power he had?

He wanted a life with me. I was torn between talking him out of it and agreeing to everything. Was there a middle way?

Someplace between him pursuing a Stateside medical career in the army and me taking off my uniform forever?

I alternated between frustration and an uncomfortable feeling of validation. *Why do I have to think about this now?* soon became *Being wanted by Caden feels too good to refuse.*

I saw him briefly in the hospital, sitting and talking to one of four guys hit by a suicide bomber. I didn't bother him. When we'd met, his compassionate side had been shut away so he could perform surgery after surgery, and I liked seeing that, somewhere in there, he had a warm heart.

"Welcome back," he whispered from behind me later as I logged a script into the computer.

"Glad to be back."

"You feeling one hundred percent?"

"Ninety-eight."

"Close enough. When do you get off?"

"Whenever you say, apparently."

"Good answer." I faced him to make sure he got the double meaning, and his smile told me he had. "See you in my bunk at nine?"

"Twenty-one hundred. On the dot."

THE LAMP GLOWED DIMLY, and the blinds were shut, but he wasn't there.

There were rose petals on the bed. I didn't know what he'd had to go through to get that many rose petals delivered to Balad Base in Fallujah in November. When I got close, I saw they were orange and purplish-red. Insane colors.

A square of paper lay on the pillow.

Naked.

A MAN OF FEW WORDS.

Languidly, I undressed, peeling off layers with increasing anticipation. Would he come in before I was through? Would he make me wait until I lay down on the bed of petals?

The trailer was heated, but the air was chilly, and my nipples twisted on themselves, hardening to erect points.

I ran my hand over the medical texts he'd brought. There were no family photos taped to the wall. No mementos or tchotchkes. He'd given me the rabbit's foot. Outside that, he was a man without sentiment.

At a soft rap on the door, I tucked myself against the wall and rapped on the window. Caden entered in scrubs and boots, closing the door.

"You're late, soldier," I said from the darkness.

He joined me in the shadows. "Complications."

He ran his finger over the little scar in my chest. It was still red and raw, messier than a surgical scar, cleaner than any shrapnel wound had business being. When he touched it, the nerve endings jumped and vibrated as if they were facing all the wrong directions.

"Ninety-eight percent," he said, letting his finger drift down to my navel.

"Give or take."

"I have to be careful with you."

"Why?"

"You don't know your own limits."

He pulled off his shirt, and I ran my hands down his chest and torso while he got his pants off, letting his erection pop out. My fist curled around his shaft, his hand stuck between my naked legs, and we kissed as if our tongues were magnetized at opposite poles. With one of my legs around his waist and my back against the wall, he put three fingers inside me. I gasped when he stretched me.

"I don't want it to hurt," he said into my cheek.

He rubbed circles around the nub of nerves inside my vagina wall.

"Doesn't hurt." My spine curved toward him as he rubbed

inside me, stimulating the spot so few could find. "Quite the"—I groaned—"contrary."

When I was barely verbal, he ran the head of his cock along my seam and slid inside, hoisting me up from behind my knees. Arms around his neck, I leaned on his shoulders as he thrust sharply, pushing me against the trailer's wood veneer. Slow, with jerking movements that pushed on my clit and the spot inside me, he brought me close, but I couldn't get over the edge. The logistics of fucking against a wall sapped my attention.

"I don't think I can like this," I groaned.

Kissing me, he reached behind him for the desk chair. He sat, slid down, and reached for me. When I went to him, he turned my back to him. I bent, impaling myself on his dick over and over. Our hands met between our legs, touching him, touching me, feeling the place we were coupled as we moved with each other.

I went blind with pleasure, speeding up with him, focusing on the hard nub where my orgasm waited.

"Can you come with me?" he asked.

"Now?"

"Yes."

"Yes."

We came together in a twist of stiffening muscles and deep-throated grunts. When his climax dripped out of me, he used it to rub me all over again.

"I can't," I said.

"Do it anyway."

With the warm liquid lubricating me, the sensation escalated all over again. I leaned my back on his chest, legs thrown over the arms of the chair as he rubbed my clit to a second orgasm.

"Stop, you're killing me," I squeaked.

He cupped his palm over my overstimulated clit. "I love it when you tell me to stop."

"That's... weird." I was still gulping for breath.

"It means I took you as far as you'll go."

"Ain't that the truth."

He got his arms under me and stood, carrying me one step to the rose-petal-covered bed.

I WAS as sleepy as I'd ever been, trying to make sense while wrapped in his arms.

"We'll get R&R when we can," I said. "ABG isn't far. Not from here."

"We'll be fine."

"For the deployment. After that... you're resigning your commission, right?"

"Yes." He peppered my face with gentle kisses. "My obligations are done."

"I don't want us to get our hopes up. The odds of us staying together—"

"Hush."

"They're not good."

"You're being a pessimist."

"I'm scared," I said, making fear my final negotiating point.

"Of what?"

"That you won't be able to stand the long distances or moving around or any of it." I didn't mention that I could retire my commission. Of the few commitments I'd ever made, the only one I could see myself sticking with was my commission.

"You don't think much of me."

"No, it's not that."

"I'm not a child, Major. I'm a grown man who can make his own decisions."

"And you're going to decide to have a life because you're normal."

"No one's ever called me that before."

"It's a compliment."

"So, a complimentary thing about me is something you're going to use to argue that we can't be together?"

I sighed and closed my eyes. "My brain can't get around what you just said."

"What I said was..." He kissed my nose. "Your thinking is incomplete. Your way of seeing me is limited. You need to give me a chance."

"Why?" I made a *mm* sound in my throat to stop his reply, waking up a little. "That came out wrong. I'm just... I want to. But outside dual deployment for married people, the army doesn't care about anyone's love life. There's no way we're going to be together much. Not for a while. I won't be surprised when you tell me you can't wait around for me."

"I'll be surprised."

"Okay. You be surprised. But I don't want to be hurt either. And, to quote a very sexy man, you can hurt me."

"I won't." He unraveled his limbs from mine and stood over me.

"Where are you going?"

"I have a shift." He got dressed, hiding his beauty from me one piece of clothing at a time. "You should stay here and get some rest. Think about it, then tell me you want me as much as I want you. Tell me you'd feel broken without me."

Asking that of me said more about how he'd feel than how I'd feel. Lying in his bed, sticky and sore, I was thrown by his need.

"I don't want to disappoint you," I said. "This life is hard, Caden. It's hard on women who grow up knowing what it's like. I can't imagine how it will be for you."

Above me, in the half light, his eyes were dark and unreadable, but his body language—the deep breath, the articulated fingers asking me to hold on, the squared shoulders—spoke of preparation to say something uncomfortable and serious.

"I'm a practical man," he said. "A surgeon has to be. If you cut somebody open and you're careless, you're going to kill them. It's not bad luck. It's not bad karma. If you're casual or cavalier about germs or how you're holding the knife, you can kill somebody. That's just the long and the short of it. So, when I met you, I figured... pheromones. Early imprinting. Reproductive instinct. You meet all the standards for beauty and then some. I'm a straight guy. My brain and my spinal cord and my dick are wired to find a female of child-bearing age. My body reacts to you because my brain releases certain hormones at the sound of your voice or the smell of apples on your skin. It's all science...until it's not."

He sat on the edge of the bed and put his shoes on, continuing as if he were describing a surgical procedure. "You know I had you down for a few fucks and a friendly good-bye. Probably about the same as you had me down for. We're adults. It's not like either one of us hasn't ever had a pheromone-induced hormone rush. But it got weird. Somewhere in those eight days when you were checking on me, it became about more than the chemicals in my brain. I panicked. I went outside the wire because I was afraid I'd lose you if I didn't. And I'm on that fucking Blackhawk, asking myself what the hell I'm doing, because the way I needed you wasn't normal. Not for a man who knows how the body and the brain affect each other."

He'd never told me what happened that night, and it looked as if that wouldn't change. He stomped his foot on the floor when he was done lacing the second boot, then he leaned over me, placing an elbow on the mattress. "I don't believe in the Universe with a capital U, and I don't believe in God. I believe in brain signals and blood. But now? I'm willing to think maybe I'm wrong about everything. This is what it comes down to. You expanded my view of the universe. I don't know what to do with that. I'm not saying I believe in fate or karma or 'meant to be' now, but my thinking got bigger because of you. I feel woken up." As if he was uncomfortable with his own feelings, he got off his elbow and hunched on the edge of the bed, looking at his laced boots. "I feel ignorant and ordinary but awake. If that means we have a long-distance relationship until you retire, then that's what it'll be."

"Okay." My voice cracked in two syllables.

"Good." He slapped his knees and stood. "Do you know when you're heading out?"

"Tomorrow afternoon."

If he was shocked by the compression of our time together, he didn't show it. "Fine. I'm off work in the morning. We'll eat, then I'll take you to the air base."

He kissed me quickly, then opened the door, letting in a blast of cold air, and shut it behind him. I heard him clop down the three wooden steps, heard his boots crunch on the rocky sand and fade into nothing.

Chapter Eight

Lunch wasn't happening.

Every scrap of paperwork had to be completed before I left, and everything had to be in order for my replacement if they decided they needed another psychiatrist.

Ronin had traveled light, so by noon, he was spending most of his remaining hours in Balad helping me clear out. He had gotten us sandwiches from the chow hall. We had the radio on as we went through the office. The amount of administrative work I'd built up in a short time was staggering.

"What's this?" Eyes wide with stories untold, he held up Pfc. Sanchez's sonogram.

I snapped it out of his hand. "Mine, that's what."

"Is there something you want to tell me?"

"Yeah. Mind your business." I put the photo in my pocket.

He held up his hands as if he wasn't now, nor had he ever, touched on the subject of the sonogram or anything else. "Should we break down the desk?"

"Someone will use it." I picked up the sandwich he'd brought. "Like me." I hoisted myself onto the desk and opened the paper on my lap.

Ronin sat next to me and opened his. "We have a nice office in ABG."

"We're sharing an office?"

You don't get far in the army without sharing, but I was a full major in a different unit, and I might need to see patients. Or not. He hadn't told me much about what I'd be doing.

"You're on loan to Army Intelligence. We're pretty much in each other's business."

I bit my sandwich. "We're clear on the other part of this offer, right?"

"The other part?"

"The you and I fucking part."

"I figured you would have mentioned it if it was on. What's keeping you? My breath? Different cologne?"

"My availability's compromised."

"Let me guess. Cap'n Fobbit."

"He went outside the wires, so you can stop that."

"He sure did." Ronin chewed his sandwich pensively.

I wiped my mouth, choosing my words carefully. "Did you hear what happened out there?"

"Yup."

"What did you hear?"

As soon as he looked at me, I knew he could tell I had no idea. He picked a limp tomato out of his sandwich and answered, "I heard he overstepped for a Haji."

Haji was a pejorative for Iraqi civilians. Maybe Caden didn't want to tell me because he thought I'd be upset with him. Maybe the whole thing had been traumatic.

"He didn't tell you." Ronin read me like a book.

Caden appeared at the door in his uniform, cap pushed back on his head. He stood there, holding a rolled-up paper plate with two sandwiches in the curl.

"Hey," I said. "Is one of those for me?"

He stepped in. "Yeah. But you have one."

"I didn't know you guys had a date." Ronin folded the paper over his sandwich and slipped off the desk.

I took one of Caden's sandwiches. "I'm pretty hungry. Thank you."

"I'm going to pack up my trailer," Ronin said. "See you on the airfield."

"See you there."

Caden held out his hand, and Ronin shook it. When he was gone, Caden sat next to me and unwrapped his lunch.

"I'm not going to sleep with him," I said.

"I know."

"Then why do you have that look on your face?"

He shrugged. "I asked to be moved up there and got a no. Flat out. No."

"You seem absolutely stunned by that."

"I've never wanted to be anywhere but where I was before. So, it's different. That's all."

We ate in silence.

"I feel guilty," I said.

"You shouldn't." He cracked open a bottle of water and set it beside me. "I'm going to figure it out."

"One man against the US Army and the woman who won't leave it."

He opened a second bottle and tipped it toward me. "I'd rather take on the army than you."

He would. He was reckless and brave, like David running after Goliath with a slingshot.

"When you went outside the wire that time?" I said. "What happened?"

He shrugged and counted on his fingers. "Brogue. A guy from Georgia and an Iraqi lady. All patched up and sent to Baghdad. Done."

"You came back barely moving."

"I had a virus that laid me up for a few days while you were in recovery." He leaned into my cheek. "That was how I got the R&R to come see you."

A virus. Possible. But the deadness in his limbs had seemed far more serious, and I didn't remember a fever, though admittedly, I hadn't checked.

I narrowed my eyes at him as if the smaller aperture would bring the truth into focus.

It did not.

MY STUFF FIT into three milk-crate-sized containers and a duffel. The bed was stripped to the mattress. I had no attachment to that or any space I'd ever occupied in my adult life.

Caden closed the door behind us. "We have half an hour," he said, putting his arms around my waist. "It's seven minutes to the airfield." He kissed my neck. "Four to board. Five or six for in-between bullshit." He pressed his pelvis into me so I could feel his erection. "Enough time."

I let out a compliant sigh. "Barely."

"I won't even undress you." He unbuckled my belt. "I'll just bend you over the desk and fuck you from behind. I want the taste of your cunt on my fingers when you leave." Fly open, pants halfway down my ass, I was already wet for him. "I want you to be sore so you're thinking of me when you land."

"I'll be thinking of you. I promise." I undid his pants, reaching in for his cock.

"Promise."

I turned away from him and leaned over the desk. He pulled my pants down to mid-thigh and kissed my bottom, leaving a trail of spit where his mouth had been. He bit the flesh. I gasped from the surprise of the lovely, light pain.

He stood behind me and ran the head of his dick along my seam, then he grabbed my hips, keeping me still enough to push inside. He ran his hand up my back and grabbed a handful of hair. "You all right?"

"Yes," I breathed.

He moved out of me slowly and thrust back in, pushing my body's limits. "I want you to think of me when you land." He yanked my hair until my face was far back enough to see him.

"I will."

"Promise."

"I promise. When we touch down, I'll say your name."

He let my hair go and curved his body along the shape of mine, reaching between my legs. "Every morning, when you wake up. Promise."

"I'll think of you first thing. I will."

He drove into me, rotating his fingers against my clit. "Before you go to sleep." He pushed so hard it hurt, and I yelped. His next was gentler. "When you're fucking yourself under the sheets."

"You," I gasped.

"You're going to come." He sped up.

I was going to come, but I couldn't get my thoughts together enough to tell him what he already knew.

"Say my name," he demanded.

"Caden."

"Every time."

"Caden."

"When you think of fucking."

"Caden, I'm..."

The orgasm ripped through me like a mortar attack, with a whistle in the air before an earth-shaking explosion that knocked me off my feet. He held me up through it, grunting like an animal as he filled me.

"Greyson," he uttered from deep in his chest. "You..." He

thrust twice more before planting his lips on the back of my neck.

I twisted around to look at him. "You too."

We kissed, and he slipped out, leaving raw soreness and satisfaction behind.

"We have three minutes," I said.

"Three and a half." Kissing me quickly on the cheek, he stood straight and slapped my ass with a crack. "Get moving, soldier."

CADEN CARRIED my duffel to the tarmac even after I insisted I was perfectly capable.

"There's no chivalry in the army," I hissed as he took it from me. "That would ruin everything."

"I'm a civilian in a uniform." He hitched the duffel strap up. "Deal with it."

The Chinook's rotors were getting started.

"God, I hate these things," I said as we walked toward it.

"Yeah." He was agreeing, but he was also staring straight at the open door where Ronin waited, which explained the single-word answer.

"I'm sore," I said as reassurance, but my words were lost in the din of helicopter blades.

Caden stopped short and dropped the duffel. I reached down to pick it up, but he put his hand on my shoulder.

"What?" I shouted. "It's not too heavy."

"Marry me."

"What?" I must have misheard in the *thupping* noise.

"Marry me, Greyson. Be my wife."

"Are you serious?" I asked, knowing full well he was dead serious.

"You said it was a unicorn assignment. You said you never heard of any one you could get out of. Well, maybe if that's the case, there's a reason for that. Maybe you shouldn't go."

I was thrown. We were supposed to kiss before I got on the helicopter and write letters and then break up.

"I can't marry you to get out of going."

"Marry me because you want to. I'll be the best husband you ever heard of. I'll take care of you. I'll stay in the army, and we can dual deploy."

"No!"

His face fell. I'd spoken too soon, but it was loud and the Phrog was waiting.

"Maybe!" Trying to make it better was making it worse. I wanted him, but he'd caught me off guard. "But you can't stay." My cap almost blew off. I had to hold it on.

"I will." The clipped demand of his voice cut through the wall of noise. "They're begging me to stay. If you don't marry me, I'm redeploying."

"Are you threatening me?"

"It's the only way to stay close to you."

"This is weird, Caden." I glanced at the helicopter.

It was ready. Ronin was waiting. The pilots were waiting.

"Marry me."

My life was waiting. But this beautiful man was waiting for me too. He was resilient and fragile, made of rock and flesh, with a strength that lunged forward only to tear him apart.

"You can't redeploy," I insisted. "That's off the table."

"Marry me, and I'll do whatever you want."

Marry him. What would I have to give up? What would I gain?

This man with strands of hair trilling in the wind and his powerful voice demanding more from me than I'd thought to give. He held me there, in his gaze, nailing my feet to the ground until I answered.

I barely knew him except by his loyalty, his passion, his vulnerability, his honesty.

I knew nothing of his life, his habits, his choices.

"Marry me. Don't go with him."

"Is this about Ronin?"

"No! I just... I have a feeling. A bad feeling about you going up there."

"You're lying."

My accusation rang more false than his denial. He wasn't lying. If his demand was about Ronin, he would have said it, and if he didn't have a feeling, that would be the last thing he'd claim. I hadn't known him that long, but I knew him that well.

"I love you, Greyson." He raised his voice as much as he had to and no more. Just enough to sound serious and straightforward. "Stay here with your unit. Marry me. I love you."

I barely knew myself or what I wanted from a man.

What was I supposed to say?

"Major!" The pilot's voice lifted over the wind.

He'd be here in a moment to hurry me away from Caden, who pinned me in place with his eyes. I'd be torn apart between the two.

His lips made the shape of words *marry me* without engaging a voice that wouldn't be heard over the sound of the Universe he didn't believe in.

Did *I* believe?

With a glance at the pilot and back to Caden's eyes, the color shaded by the brim of his cap, I answered.

Epilogue

What happened next wasn't a fairy tale. We didn't connect the dots in number order until we could see the outline of something identifiable. We made something messy, uncomfortable, distorted beyond recognition.

It was the sinking feeling you got when you feared you'd made a mistake.

It was the strength that came from knowing you only had one shot at happiness and you'd taken it.

It was looking at the face of the person who'd broken down your defenses, whom you'd shown your soft belly to, and seeing a stranger.

His proposal was the start of something I'd never expected, never wanted, never could have predicted.

After that, everything went sideways.

The Edge Series is four books.

Rough Edge | On The Edge | Broken Edge | Over the Edge
A few chapters of Rough Edge follow.

Text cdreiss to 77948 to get a message when I release something new.

FOLLOW ME ON FACEBOOK, *Twitter, Instagram, Tumblr or Pinterest.*

Join my fan groups on Facebook and Goodreads.

Get on the mailing list for deals, sales, new releases and bonus content - JOIN HERE.

My website is cdreiss.com

Rough Edge

A FEW CHAPTERS

Rough Edge
CD Reiss
The Edge - Book One
ISBN: 9781718830844
© 2018 Flip City Media Inc.
All rights reserved.

AUTHOR'S NOTE: I did research. A ton of it. But I also make stuff up for a living.

There are a thousand ways to break something and more than one method of repair. Institutions we think we know from experience have engaged thousands of others in their own, equally valid experiences. What you assume is an error may be something else entirely. Or I might have fucked up.

You can poke me with corrections on any number of subjects and if I can fix an error, I will. I'm wrong a lot.

Also, liberties were taken.

Part One

HOMECOMING

Chapter One

GREYSON
NEW YORK CITY
NOVEMBER - 2006

He was a son of a bitch, a cold-hearted compartmentalizer with a heart of solid stone. His hands were instruments of brutal precision, and his cock was a means of punishment.

He wasn't the man I'd married, but he was my husband.

I couldn't see him, even though he was kneeling between my legs. My jaw was pushed back so far, I could only see out the window next to the bed. Two fingers were jammed in my mouth. His other hand was inside my knee, pressing it to the mattress until my legs were open as far as they could go.

"Suck," he commanded with a voice drained of emotion. A flat order, like "sit" or "heel."

I curved my lips around the fingers and sucked on them. They tasted of rubbing alcohol and pussy.

"Harder."

I sucked harder and he pushed my jaw up, restraining me with my position. He ran his other hand from my knee to the inside of my thigh. When he got to the fleshiest part, he tightened his grip until pain blossomed under his fingers and grew outward, lacing my arousal with its companion—pain.

When he let go, I whimpered around his fingers, and he responded by pushing them deeper down my throat. As he leaned over me, I felt his rod of an erection where I was wet.

He whispered into my cheek, "Take them. All the way." I opened my throat and he pushed his fingers down. "Beg for it."

I couldn't speak with his fingers in my mouth. I couldn't even breathe.

"You're not begging." His fingers were down to the webs and my body contracted around them for air. He pulled them out. "Beg."

"Fuck me. Please fuck me."

"What?" With his spit-soaked hand, he reached between my legs and pinched my swollen clit.

"Put your cock in me. Fuck me hard. Take what you want. Please. Please." The last word came as a whisper.

He got on his knees, magnificent, cut like a god from jaw to abs to the hard heat of his thighs. One hand on my sternum to hold me still, the other guiding his cock between my legs. I was so wet, open like a hungry flower, still whispering *please please please* as he leaned his weight on my chest and drove into me. He was long and thick. Without prep, he could hurt me, and he did.

I knew when to look for the change. I knew how to see him recover himself in the violence. In the moment he drove through me so hard he cracked, went supple, and became my husband again.

The first orgasm came on the third thrust and lasted until he joined me in heaven.

GREYSON
FORT BRAGG
AUGUST - 1992

BASIC TRAINING WAS A CAKEWALK. Last course. Blue group did belly robber, high step over, low wire, weaver, and island hopper. Halfway through, I fell fifteen feet off the confidence climb. I thought I'd wiped out for good with my full weight on my right wrist and the rest of the blue group's boots smacking the mud all around me.

"Get up, you little fucking shit!"

Ronin.

That was Ronin yelling, and Ronin grabbing me under the

arms to throw me toward the next obstacle.

"Move it!" He pushed me. "I'm staying behind you, so if you go pussy, you're answering to me!"

I tucked my wrist under my breasts, dropped to my knees and crawled under the low wire. He was behind me, shouting a litany of encouragements and insults. I climbed the wall with one hand and my teeth and stumbled over the line in the middle of the pack, aching, bruised, tears streaking the mud on my face. Ronin was at attention behind me.

"That doesn't look like attention, Frazier!" Sergeant Bell shouted.

I put my right arm to my side and straightened my wrist. Pain shot through to my shoulder, but still, I stood at attention. Bell didn't seem satisfied.

"You're up shit creek now, Private One More."

"Fuck you, Ronin."

Bell stormed to me, hands clasped behind his back, nearly crashing into Rodrigo, who was trying to get into the line. Rodrigo buckled and found his space. Bell was not deterred. I put my eyes at attention and tried to tamp down the heavy breaths. Everything hurt. I felt as if I'd flung myself out of a moving car, but I stood still.

When Bell got uncomfortably close, I expected him to shout, but he murmured two words so low, only I could hear them.

"Stop smiling."

Chapter Two

GREYSON · SEPTEMBER, 2006

The sky in Iraq was the bluest blue I'd ever seen. It had a flat depth, as if thin layers of glass, each a slightly different shade, were stacked together. Sometimes I'd dream about that sky. Either I'd be floating in it, blue everywhere, above and below, at each side and pressure point, squeezing the breath out of me, or I'd be falling from it, from blue into blue, no Earth barreling into greater and greater detail. Just a single direction in the never-ending cerulean sky.

Caden and I had been separated by an ocean and a war for ten months. We'd married while I was on leave and spoke when our schedules matched and the wind blew the wi-fi signal in the right direction. I thought I hadn't known him long enough to miss him, but I did.

Painfully. Tenderly. Thoroughly. Our separation stretched the bond between us to a thin, translucent strand, but did not break it.

Caden's eyes had the color and layered depth of the Iraqi sky.

When I missed him, I looked up. When I wrapped his T-shirt around my neck, my dreams of the blue sky lost their nightmarish edge, and the bond became a little less taut.

Jenn and I flew to New York in our uniforms. She remained on active duty and had a job waiting at the VA Hospital in Newark. I had a husband and no job.

"You want to put on some makeup or something?" she asked.

"Why? You afraid they're all looking at me?"

The crew had moved us to first class. I craned my neck to see a jowly businessman sleeping with his mouth open. A mid-level rap star with cornrows and a name I couldn't recall was reading a book to his daughter, and two middle-aged women chatted in the row across. No one was giving my lashes the side-eye.

"Hell, no. But maybe you want to look nice for your husband?" She rooted around a quilted pink bag and found a black stick. "Here. Lip gloss."

"It's only going to wind up on his dick."

She burst out laughing and replaced the lip gloss with mascara. "Here. Doll it up just a little. You're a civilian now."

I took the mascara, and she handed me a compact with a mirror. I flipped it open and looked at myself in circular sections.

I was a civilian now.

I had no idea how to be that.

———————

AS THE ONLY girl in a military family, enlisting wasn't encouraged. It wasn't unexpected either. It made them proud. And disappointed. And worried. A mixed bag of emotions that probably had nothing to do with either parent and everything with how I felt at every time I wondered what they thought.

I would have stayed in the army my entire life, but Caden happened, and he saw the army as his duty to the country. A debt to pay, not a way of life.

At the gate, a little girl of about six ran up and gave Jenn and me flowers. "Thank you for your service," she said.

This wasn't uncommon. I'd learned people were in awe of my career choice and the risks it involved.

I kneeled and took the flowers. "Thank you for the flowers. And thank you for appreciating us. That means a lot."

Suddenly shy, she curtsied and ran away to her mother, who waved at me. I gave her a thumbs-up.

"Is it wrong to wish she was a single, six foot-tall black man with a nice bank account?" Jenn asked quietly, sniffing the flowers.

"Her mother might be a little surprised."

Jenn chuckled and pointed at the sign above. "Baggage claim, this way."

We didn't get two steps before I saw Caden waiting for me. He had flowers tied with stars and stripes printed on the ribbon, a grey suit, and smile that told me he saw me the way I saw him—with a certain amount of surprise at the easy familiarity, and another bit of gratitude at the fulfilled expectations. It was as if we were seeing each other for the first time, and coming back to something very familiar.

I dropped my bag and ran into his arms. We clung to each other, connected in a kiss that held nothing back. Cocooned, shielded by love and commitment, the airport terminal fell behind the wall of our attention to the kiss.

He jerked me away with a sucking sound and a drawn breath, but kept his nose astride mine. "Welcome to New York, Major."

That was when I heard the applause.

"Are we making a spectacle of ourselves?" I let my body relax away from his.

"I fucking love you so much, I don't even care."

I looked at the people surrounding us. I was in camo and he had a flag ribbon on the flowers. We were indeed making a spectacle of ourselves.

Jenn dropped my bag at my feet. "That was so sweet I almost clapped."

Caden took it before I could. "Thank you for not."

The crowd dispersed, and we headed out of baggage claim without further incident.

"WHAT DO you want to see first?" Caden asked after we dropped Jenn off at her parents' brownstone in Fort Greene. His wrist was draped over the steering wheel of his Mercedes. The band of his expensive watch caught glints of the sun. The seats were soft black leather. There was no dust or sand on the carpets, and none of the upholstery was torn.

"The inside of my eyelids."

"Come on, Major. Push on." He squeezed my knee and kissed me at the red light. "You'll sleep when you're dead."

I put my hand over his, and he stroked my thumb. "Were your eyes always this blue?"

"Probably."

They looked bluer against the New York sky, which was fluffed with late summer clouds. I sat back and looked out the window. Maybe tomorrow I'd see the color I'd fall through.

"What are my choices?" I asked.

"The house, your new office, or any restaurant in the city."

That was more choices than I was used to, and none involved getting sand in the crack of my ass or telling a man it was okay to kill people.

"Can we eat in?"

"Yep."

The seams in the bridge's surface went *puh-puh-puh* under the tires and the web of cables holding it up blurred in my peripheral vision. Manhattan stretched ahead of me like a dense construction of grey bricks. I didn't know where people fit into such compactness.

"Okay," I finally said. "The house."

CADEN PUT the car in a garage a block away. Apparently he'd bought the spot years ago. It required a mortgage and operating fees. Where I grew up, you parked in a lot someone else owned, your own driveway, or on the street.

This was my new normal.

On the walk along Columbus Avenue, I felt as if I were wearing a camo clown suit. Caden put his arm around me and kissed my temple as we waited at the light. The crowd crossed before the light changed to green, but I followed my husband.

"We're on 87th between Columbus and Amsterdam," he said. "Avenues run north-south, streets run east-west."

"Got it." We turned onto a narrow, tree-lined street. "This is a nice block."

"It is."

The houses were stone and connected to each other on the sides. Some were slightly set back from the street to accommodate a stoop and a few steps down to a garden apartment.

He stopped by one such house and held his hand out while the other took my duffel off his shoulder. "Here we are."

I looked up. Garden apartment. Three stories. An attic with stone carvings around the leaded windows. "Is it all yours?"

He threw the duffel up the steps. It made it halfway. "It's all ours."

He picked me up in his arms before carrying me up the stoop. I squeaked in surprise. We laughed as he tried to unlock the door without dropping me, and when he managed to do it, I cheered.

He retrieved my bag and dropped it in the foyer. We were at the base of a flight of stairs. Everything was polished dark wood carved at the corners. A beveled mirror was set into a frame with three brass hooks under it. I took off my cap and let my hair fall.

I was fully overwhelmed. He took my cap and put it on a hook before taking my face in his hands and kissing me.

"I have your back," he whispered. "Okay?" I nodded, and he kissed me again. "Say it for me."

"You have my back."

"And your front."

I smiled into his kiss. "You have my front."

"I can take you to the bedroom if you insist or on the stairs right now."

"Will you give me a minute to shower?"

"You have rank."

"That's an order then."

He got his hips under me and his hands under my ass, hitching me up until I could get my legs around his waist. He carried me to our room. I didn't see anything but his face on the way up. I only knew there were wood floors and windows. Two flights. A tower with me on top.

HE SAT me on a bench in the bathroom and turned the water on in the white claw-foot tub. He kneeled in front of me to unlace my boots. I couldn't stop looking at him in his fancy suit, kneeling on the bathroom floor to service me.

"I hate that they make us wear this shit on the way home," he said. "It's total PR."

"Yeah, well, the military is nothing without its symbols, and that's what I am."

"Were." He pulled off the boot. "Now you are Dr. Greyson Frazier, MD, with a psychiatric practice in Manhattan." He peeled off my socks. "And my wife. Stand up."

Still on his knees, he undid my buckle and fly and pulled my pants down, letting his palms spread out over the skin of my thighs. I stepped out of them and he tossed the pants aside.

"Ah, I missed this." He lifted my shirt and kissed the silver scar over my heart. He kissed my belly and the triangle below. I put my fingers in his hair, and he reached up under my clothes until he found my hardened nipples.

"Caden," I groaned. "Bath."

With a gentle suck on my belly, he stood. I started unbuttoning from the top and he unbuttoned from the bottom. We met in the middle and got all my clothes off until I wasn't wearing anything but the dog tags that hung between my breasts.

He laid them in his palm and looked at them, letting one clink against the other.

"Take them off," I said.

He closed his fist around them and pulled them over my head. The chain slid against my long, straight hair, and I was free.

Caden coiled the chain on the vanity. I shut off the water and tested it.

Scalding hot.

No one in the world knew me the way he did.

HE'D TAKEN his jacket off, rolled up his sleeves, and bathed me, touching every part of my body. His hands knew exactly how to tease me. They were accurate and subtle, driving my desire forward without letting me come.

He tossed the towel away and threw me on the bed, soaking wet.

He didn't even undress to fuck me. Not right away. He just spread my legs and slid his fingers inside me, then took out his monster of a cock and fucked me as if we hadn't seen each other in four months.

The sheets were white.

The furniture was honey, and the lamps were Tiffany.

Day turned into evening, but the street didn't quiet.

That was all I noticed between orgasms.

In the darkness, we curled under the covers. He stroked my arm with his thumb, appreciating every inch of skin.

"I haven't shown you the house," he said. "I'm sorry."

"Are you going to show me all your childhood secret hiding places?"

"The speakeasy in the basement? Yes."

He'd told me about the Prohibition-era space the first owners had dug out of the basement. How it had false walls, a mosaic tile floor, a mahogany bar, and secret places to hide customers and almost a century later, small children.

"It's a really nice house," I said. "Is this a good neighborhood, as neighborhoods go in New York?"

"This block is unattainable."

"What's that mean?"

"This house is priceless. I could name a number and get it."

"Your dad was smart to buy it when he did."

"He wanted to be near enough to the hospital, but not that close. He had a space for a practice in the garden apartment, which is soon to be..." He waited for me to finish.

"My practice."

"Bingo."

"I'm nervous."

"I know."

"What if I—"

He put his finger on my lips before I could utter my litany of doubts. "You're going to do fine. And if it takes longer than you think it should, we can survive on a heart surgeon's salary for a while."

Of course we could. There was nothing to be nervous about. He had my back and my front.

"Can I see the office?"

"Yes."

WE WIGGLED into pajamas and went down the back stairs, which led to a short carpeted hall with an old wooden door at each end.

"The door at the back leads to a shared kind of alley thing out the front, so patients won't bump into each other on the way in and out," Caden said as he turned the skeleton key that stuck out of the office's keyhole. It clacked deeply before the door swung open. He flicked on the lights.

The office defied every expectation.

I expected cold fluorescents and a dropped ceiling.

What I got was a pristine white ceiling and warm lamps.

I expected an empty space.

What I got was a 1950s era desk and chairs, tufted couch, end tables, a clock where I could see it but the patient couldn't, and a deep blue carpet to muffle the distracting scrape of chairs and footsteps. Behind the desk, a horizontal filing cabinet had framed pictures leaning on the top. Family. Friends. Caden and me on the rooftop of the hotel in Amman, with the sunset behind us. I picked up our wedding photo. My parents had set up the backyard in flowers and tables, doing the best they could when they heard we were getting hitched on two-day leave. Caden and me outside the combat hospital in Balad, dressed in dull green and smiles.

"I read up on what you'd need. They said family pictures humanized you to patients."

"That's right."

He opened the door on the far end of the room. The waiting room was bathed in the same warm lamplight. It was small. Two chairs and a love seat. A coffee table. A Wasily Kandinski print. Everything matched the interior office.

"I had speakers put in." He pointed up. Small wood-grain boxes hung in the corners where the ceiling met the walls. "I hear music soothes the savage breast."

Caden, a psychiatrist's husband, had hang-ups about mental illness that had revealed themselves after I accepted his proposal.

"I won't be working with savages," I said with a raised eyebrow. I was going to have to patiently whittle away this particular neurosis.

"They won't all have breasts either." He put his arm around me. "So you like it?"

"I love it. Madly, deeply. I love it." I put my arms around his shoulders, and his snaked around my waist. "Thank you so much."

"There's so much we're going to do together." He kissed my neck. "We're going to build an entire life out of a war."

"That would be a miracle."

"First of many. You and me. We're a miracle." He pulled back so he could see my face. "You know what I see when I look at you?"

"Your wife?"

"The worst decisions I've ever made, I made for a reason. You. You rose out of the destruction. Our life together will be built into the best from what survived the worst."

"That's very poetic."

He smiled. "I've been thinking about what to say for days. I wanted to explain how magnificent we're going to be."

"Magnificent?"

"I don't think I quite nailed it." He took me back into the hall and to an unremarkable door under the stairs. "Basement."

He opened the door, and flicked on the light. Wooden stairs led to a dirt floor in a four-by-five room. Caden reached around me and put his hands on a vase sitting on a set-in shelf. He yanked it, and the wall slid to the side, revealing a mosaic floral floor and dark wood bar stacked high with cardboard boxes.

"Chez Columbus," he said, smiling. "1925-1933."

Amazing. An actual speakeasy with a stairway to the hidden alley on the side of the house, hidden rooms, and lastly, behind the laundry room, a big wall safe. He opened it, then pushed away the wall behind it to yet another room with cylindrical holes in the concrete.

"The bottle room," he said. "This was where I hid when... you know."

"When you were scared."

"When I should have been stopping him from beating her."

"I'm going to get you out of the habit of blaming yourself."

"Good luck." He held out his hand, moving the subject away from the abuse of his mother as he always did. "Come on. It's cold in here."

The steps to the bedroom seemed like an eternal climb, but we wound up racing to the top. It didn't matter who won. We both landed on the bed.

We held each other tight, and I felt safe starting a new life with him.

THAT NIGHT, with the *whoosh* of cars outside and a police siren whining far away, he woke with a grunt and a command. "Stop!"

I reached for my revolver, but it was locked away in a strange closet, in the strange bedroom, in a city that was a sea of stone.

But he was there, the street light blue on his cheek, and all was well as long as he was next to me.

"Caden? Are you okay?"

"Yeah." He rolled over to face me. "Sorry."

"What was it?"

"Dream. Nothing."

PTSD was as real as the war itself, and I had to know if he was reliving it in his sleep. "Caden. Can you tell me?"

"Pieces of me were breaking off."

"Were you in Iraq? In the dream?"

"No." His denial was barely a whisper.

I took it for a normal nightmare and joined him in sleep.

Get the next book - *Rough Edge* today!

THE WHOLE SERIES will be out in a short timeframe.

Cutting Edge | Rough Edge | On The Edge | Broken Edge | Over the Edge

Also by CD Reiss

The Edge Series

Rough. Edgy. Sexy enough to melt your device.

Cutting Edge | Rough Edge | On The Edge | Broken Edge | Over the Edge

The Submission Series

Jonathan brings out Monica's natural submissive.

Submission | Domination | Connection

Corruption Series

Their passion will set the Los Angeles mafia on fire.

SPIN | RUIN | RULE

Forbidden Series

Fiona has 72 hours to prove she isn't insane. Her therapist has to get through three days without falling for her.

KICK | USE | BREAK

Contemporary Romances

Hollywood and sports romances for the sweet and sexy romantic.

Shuttergirl | Hardball | Bombshell | Bodyguard

Made in the USA
Lexington, KY
14 June 2018